PRAISE FOR JOSH LANYON

"Josh Lanyon doesn't just top the A-List -- he IS the A-List when it comes to blending wit, suspense and romance."

Lily for Romance Junkies Reviews
– A Blue Ribbon Rating

"Josh Lanyon has penned another wonderful novel that completely engrossed me in from the first page. Fabulous world building coupled with deep, rich history and a great lead character had me glued to my eReader for much of our very rainy Easter Sunday. Lanyon is such a skilled writer, so talented that I wonder if there isn't a genre where he wouldn't excel.

Lynn for Reviews by Jessewave

"Nuances of gestures and dialogue are two things Josh Lanyon does as well or better than anyone. He builds the characters in a way that keeps us from being sure what direction he'll take us. If his books had a soundtrack behind it we'd be sitting waiting for that noise that indicates bad things are coming. There's great eroticism blended well into any Josh Lanyon book. This one is no exception as dreams lead into some powerful and intense sexual activity. Lanyon remains at the top of my list for great storytelling with a thrilling finale."

The Romance Studio

"Josh Lanyon is one of those authors who, regardless of the story, always tells a captivating tale that draws the reader right in."

Kathy K., Reviews at Ebook Addict

STRANGER THINGS HAVE HAPPENED
An Adrien English Write Your Own Damn Story

December 2013, JustJoshin Publishing, Inc.

ISBN-10: 1-937909-44-1
ISBN-13: 978-1-937909-44-4

Published in the United States of America

JustJoshin Publishing, Inc.
3053 Rancho Vista Blvd.
Suite 116
Palmdale, CA 93551
www.joshlanyon.com

DEDICATION

For everyone who loves and misses Adrien and Jake. Not the novel you were hoping for, I know, but I hope you will have as many laughs — and perhaps a few tears — reading these crazy adventures as I did writing them.

STRANGER THINGS HAVE HAPPENED

An Adrien English Write Your Own Damn Story

JOSH LANYON

WARNING!!!

This is a work of fiction. Even more so than usual.

If you have never encountered gamebooks or Choose Your Own Adventure stories, then there are some things you should know. First of all, though it is based on the original novel Fatal Shadows, you can't read this story through from beginning to end. It won't make sense. It might not make sense anyway. As you read, you will be asked to make choices as to what the characters should do next.

Some of the choices will be trivial, insignificant. Some will be momentous. You won't know ahead of time which is which. Some choices will lead you in circles. Some will lead to <u>dead ends</u>. Some will lead to quiet residential cul-de-sacs with white picket fences and teenagers who play the music too loud. Some will lead to danger and death. Or worse.

If you prefer to stick to Adrien English's original choices, you are free to follow the breadcrumbs. We promise not to make chicken noises or flap our arms at you.

Choose wisely! Your success in unraveling the mystery of who killed Robert Hersey will depend completely on YOU!

Cops before breakfast. Before coffee even.
As if Mondays aren't bad enough.

After last night it's not a total surprise.

Oh, but first things first. You are a thirty-two-year-old Los Angeles bookstore owner. You're reasonably successful despite the fact that these are hard times for indie bookstores, and you recently sold your first novel *Murder Will Out* to a small press. That's about it for your professional life. Your personal life...well, you don't have a personal life, let's face it.

Your college sweetheart walked out years ago because you've got a bum ticker and he didn't want to take a chance on getting saddled with, well, you. Not that he didn't love you and everything.

Did I mention you are gay?

Anyway.

Cops. Standing outside Cloak and Dagger Books at this very second — crowding the welcome mat and leaning on the buzzer.

For God's sake. It's not even seven in the morning. Whatever this is, it's not good news.

You stumble downstairs, shove back the ornate security gate, unlock the glass front doors, and let them in: two plainclothes detectives.

They identify themselves with a show of badges. Detective Chan is older, paunchy, a little rumpled, smelling of Old Spice and cigarettes as he brushes by you. The other one, Detective Riordan, is big and blond, with a neo-Nazi haircut and tawny eyes. Your gut clenches as you meet those cold, light eyes. Call it instinct. Call it premonition.

"I'm afraid we have some bad news for you, Mr. English," Detective Chan says.

You already know what he's going to say. His face — that professionally neutral expression — is a giveaway. You don't risk another look at Riordan. He makes you nervous though you're not normally the nervous type. You head for your office in the back of the bookstore, and you keep walking as Chan finishes, "...concerning an employee of yours. A Mr. Robert Hersey."

The cops tell you that Robert, who in addition to being your employee is your oldest — and once closest — friend, has been stabbed to death in the alley behind his West Hollywood apartment.

That's the bad news. There is no good news. They start asking you questions about your relationship with Robert. You stick to the bare facts as much as possible and volunteer no information. You've been selling mystery novels long enough to know that much.

"Were you lovers?" Chan glances at Riordan. Riordan must be the guy in charge.

"No."

"But you *are* homosexual?" Riordan never blinks, his gaze never veers.

"I'm gay. What of it?"

"And Hersey was homosexual?" In a minute they're going to bring up the argument at the Blue Parrot. You consider refusing to answer any more questions without your lawyer present. But that's liable to look guilty, right? That's what the cops on TV always say.

You keep fencing and they keep probing, trying to find the weak spot in your defense, and then finally — FINALLY — they leave, promising to keep in touch. That's copspeak for *you're not fooling anyone, English*. Before he walks out the door, that asshole Riordan picks up an empty Tab can and throws it in the wrong trash bin. Well, when you own the entire fucking planet, you don't need to worry about recycling.

You hear the phone in your office ringing as you relock the glass front doors and drag the ornate security gate across the entrance. If you had a few planks of solid oak and a handful of nails, you'd board the place up.

But no sooner do you get that heavy old gate into place than a dark-haired woman in a yellow raincoat starts pounding on the glass doors.

"We're not open yet," you mouth to her.

"Mr. English! It's me. Mariah Packard."

Who the...?

4

Mariah reminds you that you agreed to include Cloak and Dagger bookstore as a stop on one of those morbid murder tours. Way back in the thirties, no, the forties — or was it the fifties? — anyway, way back before you were even a gleam in your old man's eye, this building was a hotel called The Huntsman's Lodge. A hotel where, according to urban legend, a murder took place.

But wait a minute. When did you agree to be part of a creepy tourist attraction? You never agreed to that! No way. Not your style.

It doesn't matter. This is the way the story is heading, so roll with it.

Once more you drag the security gate back and open the glass doors. A group of middle-aged Midwesterner types file in, looking google-eyed and awestruck. Have these people never seen books before? Do they spend all their free time eating fructose-based foods and watching dance competition shows on TV?

Mariah asks where the murder took place. She means the OTHER murder, clearly, since poor Rob was killed in West Hollywood. You tell the tour guide that her guess is as good as yours, and you retreat to your office.

If you decide to immediately call your lawyer,
turn to page 7

If you change your mind and decide a shower
and some coffee would be a good idea,
turn to page 16

Claude is so kind and so persistent — and you so desperately don't want to move in with your mother — that eventually you let yourself be persuaded to move in with him when you're finally released from rehab.

Claude lives in a small pink bungalow in Los Feliz, which he spares no effort preparing for you. During the day and a lot of the evening, Claude is at Café Noir. His mother comes in to take care of you. She's a big, gruff woman with a strong back and a stronger stomach. Why it's easier to let Claude's mother care for you, than your own, is one of life's mysteries. It's not like Lisa would be the one actually feeding and changing you. Anyway, despite Lisa's dire predictions, you survive. In fact, you and Mrs. La Pierra quickly grow fond of each other.

Claude takes care of you when he's home in the evenings and at night. Maybe it helps that you've always been completely honest with each other, and that you've both got a sense of humor. At first you sleep in a hospital bed in the tiny guest bedroom. There's barely enough room for the bed, your wheelchair, and Mrs. La Pierra's old sewing machine. You watch the moon slipping through the fingers of the orange tree in the backyard. You listen to the stray cats fighting and mating.

The nights are very long. You have too much time to think of what could have been...

6

But Claude was right, love does eventually come — as does acceptance.

One day, as you sit in the garden, feeling the sun on your face and listening to the birds singing, you realize that you're glad you're alive. You're even happy.

Claude's also right about you being good at business, even if your first crazed impulse was to open a bookstore. Together, aided by your mother's generous financial backing, the two of you turn Café Noir into one of the hottest restaurants in Los Angeles.

At your urging, Mrs. La Pierra takes a couple of night courses and eventually she becomes your personal assistant. You resume your publishing career and your sixth book actually goes to #1 on the New York Times bestseller list. British actor Paul Kane eventually options it for a movie.

The End

Hands shaking, you dial the family lawyer, elderly Mr. Gracen of Hitchcock & Gracen. Except it's just past nine in the morning, right? So you get the firm's answering machine. This is not exactly something you can explain over the phone — and you don't want to try lest Mr. Gracen stop taking your phone calls.

You hang up and the phone rings again.

"Adrien, *mon chou*," flutes the high, clear voice of your friend, Claude La Pierra.

Claude owns Café Noir on Hillhurst Ave. He's big and black and beautiful. You've known him for a couple of years — you met when you were still going to those organized gay singles outings, back before you figured out that it was easier being lonely on your own than in a group. Claude loves all things French and has even taught himself the language. Well, *un peu.*

"I just heard," he continues. "It's too ghastly. I still can't believe it. Tell me I'm dreaming."

If only that were the case. "The police just left."

"The police? *Mon Dieu!* What did they say? Do they know who did it?"

"I don't think so." You're not sure now whether that's a good thing or a bad thing.

"What did they tell you? What did you tell them? Did you tell them about me?"

8

Claude invites you to lunch. Which sounds more festive than it is. Claude wants the scoop on the murder investigation and he wants to compare notes. Claude's an amazing cook, but this sounds like a recipe for indigestion.

If you agree to go to Café Noir for lunch,
turn to page 23

If you decide to stay in and work through lunch,
turn to page 25

If you decide to go back to bed and start this day over,
turn to page 10

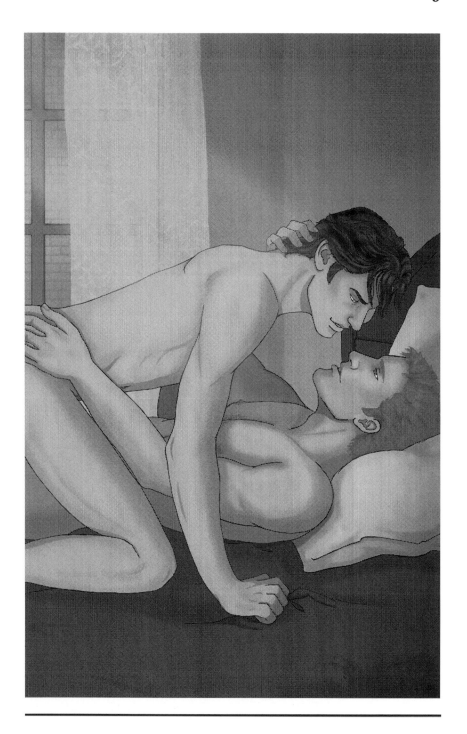

No, YOU CANNOT GO BACK TO BED AND START THE DAY OVER. Come on, man up! The story is moving now, it's too late to stop it. You know that. If you keep standing there with the deer-in-the-headlights look, it's going to roll right over you.

Let's try this again.

If you decide to go to lunch at Claude's,
turn to page 23

If you decide to call your ex-boyfriend Mel because
you're feeling scared and lonely and you
suddenly just want to hear his voice,
turn to page 19

If you decide to just skip to the part where
you and Detective Riordan have sex,
turn to page 9

From a lateral recess shoot two enormous tentacles — black, wavy as serpents, covered with hair, armed at the extremity with a strong double claw.

(Editor's note: It might be useful to pause here and explain that "lateral recess" refers to a cave in a nameless African jungle and not any particular person's anatomy.)

Anywho, the enormous tentacles reach forth noiselessly to within a couple of yards of where you stand, then two more follow with a quick, wavy jerk. And now behind these, a head, as large as that of a man, black, hairy, bearing a strange resemblance to the most awful and cruel human face ever stamped with the devil's image — whose dull, goggle eyes, fix on the appalled ones of its discoverer — that would be you, though it's easy to see how you might have forgotten in this endless stream of WORDS — seeming to glow and burn with a truly diabolical glare.

Wait. What was the question?

You stand staring into the countenance of this awful thing. Your blood curdles to ice within you. Is it the Fiend himself who takes such unknown and fearful shape to appear before you here in the gloom of this foul and loathsome cavern? Then, as your eyes grow more and more used to the dim shades, you make out a huge body crouching back in the recess, half hidden by a quivering mass of black, hairy tentacles.

Eww. When the hell does Jake show up?

12

For a few moments you stand there — WHY? — then with a cry of horror you throw out your hand to ward off an attack. One wouldn't expect that to be very useful, but the four tentacles already protruding are quickly withdrawn, and the fearful creature, whatever it is, seems to shrink back into the cranny. One last look upon the hairy heap of moving, writhing horror — upon these dreadful red demon eyes, and you, who have faced death again and again without shrinking, must struggle to resist the impulse to turn and flee. You do resist, of course, because people are watching — yet it is with flesh shuddering and knees trembling beneath you that you retreat, step by step, backwards, until you stand once more in the full light of day.

Vampire — insect — devil — what is this thing? From the length and thickness of those frightful tentacle-like legs (or leg-like tentacles), stretching forth from the cranny, you — who have (as previously mentioned) oft times faced down death but are currently running full steam ahead until you gain the ridge dividing the hollow — estimate that the creature, when spread out, must be eight or ten feet in diameter.

You look back. IT has not followed you from the cave. Why?

At this juncture of your meditations your mind becomes alive to two discoveries — one, that you have gained the farther end of the ridge; the other, that immediately before and beneath you, just over the slope of the ridge, lies the body of a man.

Uh oh.

Uh. Oh.

Cautiously, you set down the bag with the burger and fries on the floor.

From the sounds of destruction, it doesn't appear that the intruder or intruders have noticed that the side door is standing wide open — or that the delicious aroma of fast food is now filling the shop.

Quietly, very quietly, you sneak down the nearest aisle of bookshelves, picking your way over the tumbled books and broken vases and smashed statues. If you can get to the faux fireplace in the back, there is a very real poker you could use as a weapon.

You duck down as you reach a section of shelving where all the books have been knocked out, leaving a makeshift window between the canyons of shelves. You crouch down and continue to the end of the shelving unit. You risk a glance around the corner. You can see the fireplace, but the poker is nowhere in sight.

Shit! Now what?

Suddenly it is dead silent in the bookstore. Not so much as the scrape of a page disturbs that unnatural hush. The hair rises on the nape of your neck.

It's only too likely the intruder or intruders have belatedly noticed they are not alone! Your only chance now is to get out while you can.

You turn around to make your way back the way you came, but a giant shadow looms up over you. You only have a second to stare into the empty brown eyes of a complete stranger before the poker comes crashing down on your head.

Unfortunately, your overstrained heart can't take this double shock. Crushing pain settles on your chest and you struggle for breath as you fall back on a mound of noir fiction. A pair of immaculate loafers steps into your line of vision. A deep voice speaks from overhead, but you can't make out the words. Just before your vision dims and grows dark, you remember your mother telling you fast food would be the death of you...

The End

16

As you reach the upstairs landing, you realize you didn't bother to lock your living quarters when you went downstairs to greet LAPD's finest, and now two members of that crazy tour group are wandering around your apartment.

That's a little unsettling. Through the open bedroom door, you can see a heavyset woman pawing through your underwear drawer. Meanwhile, there's an elderly man in a blue Hawaiian shirt tugging on the bookcase in the living room. He has sparse jet-black hair, a pencil-thin mustache, and a camera around his neck. In a minute he's going to yank the shelves out of the wall.

"Can I help you?" you ask, and he jumps a foot.

Out of the corner of your eye, you see the woman in the bedroom slam shut the drawer and head for your bathroom. Holy moly!

The elderly man clears his throat. "I was just examining the workmanship on this bookshelf. It's very fine. Yes sirree, a very fine piece of carpentry indeed. Mahogany, isn't it?"

You have your faults, but bad manners are not one of them. "I'm sorry, Mr. er...?"

"Harrison. Henry Harrison." Mr. Harrison smiles with wide and open friendliness."

I'm sorry, Mr. Harrison," you say, "but these rooms are not part of the tour."

"Is that so?" Mr. Harrison's smile fades and he looks very disappointed. "But this is all part of the original structure, isn't it?"

Yes, the upstairs rooms were all part of the original structure, but they are still not part of the tour. You explain all this politely, and Mr. Harrison finally exits stage left. You hover in your bedroom doorway waiting for the lady in the bathroom to finish up. Finally you hear the sound of the toilet flushing, the sink running, and the door knob turning.

The door opens and a woman with dark frizzy hair steps out. She smiles politely, but offers no explanation as she scoots past you and heads for the hall and the bookstore entrance.

You open your mouth to...well, to do what? This is such a weird, unhappy day. What's one more weirdness? Besides, you can hear Mariah clucking after her straying chicks.

You see the lady with the frizzy hair safely out of your apartment and downstairs. As you reach the ground level, you notice Henry Harrison examining the paneling behind the faux fireplace, and he offers a guilty smile as he spots you. Mariah calls time and the tour departs as unceremoniously as they arrived. You lock the door firmly behind the last stragglers, ignoring grumbles that Cloak and Dagger Books was a letdown. There are days you would even agree.

Back upstairs, you shower, dress, fix yourself coffee and head downstairs once more to reopen the shop. You call the temp agency you used to use before Robert returned from the Heartland and started working for you. They promise to send someone.

You hope it's soon because the quiet is already getting on your nerves.

No sooner do you think this than the phone rings again. This time it's a reporter: Bruce Green from *Boytimes*.

If you decide to talk to Bruce Green,
turn to page 29

If you decide you're hungry and you might as well
take Claude up on his offer of lunch,
turn to page 23

If you decide to just skip to the part where
you and Detective Riordan have se — oops!
If you decide to work a while longer and
then grab some fast food,
turn to page 25

Seriously? *Mel?* Okay. It's your funeral.

(I hope that's just a figure of speech, but after all, this is a Choose Your Own Adventure story.)

You catch Mel, who happens to teach film studies at UC Berkeley, in his office between classes.

"Hello, stranger," Mel says, his warm voice growing even warmer.

You chat briefly and then you tell him about Robert. Mel is naturally horrified. Er, naturally Mel is horrified. (Although horror was all too frequently a natural state for him during your years together, come to think of it.) He's even more horrified to hear that you seem to be a suspect in the investigation. This is the kind of thing Mel's parents warned him about. Well, no. You actually *don't* seem like the kind of person to get involved in a murder investigation, but they always knew you'd be trouble.

But to give Mel credit, he doesn't seem to doubt for a second that you're innocent. He even asks what he can do to help.

You realize there really isn't anything he can do. Not now. You start to feel self-conscious about calling him. You wind up the phone call quickly despite your impression that Mel wants to keep chatting.

Before you hang up, Mel asks, "Are you taking care of yourself, Adrien?"

"Of course. Always." You try not to sound testy.

"Are you —? Have you —?"

Found someone? "It's complicated," you lie. What's complicated about being alone and lonely? "Are you still with Phil?"

"Paul," Mel corrects gently.

"Right. The former student."

"Former grad student." Mel's voice is extremely neutral. "Things are okay."

Yeah, clearly not. And you can't help feeling bitter satisfaction.

Happy now, you goof?
Turn to page 23

Robert's apartment is not sealed yet. No official yellow tape stretches across the front door proclaiming it a crime scene. Does that mean the cops haven't had time to sift through Robert's things? Is it possible they could be that sloppy? That slow? That gimlet-eyed Detective Riordan doesn't seem like the type to overlook anything.

You hesitate on the walkway, listening to the palm fronds flapping in the breeze and the dull roar of the nearby Hollywood Freeway. Nobody seems to be around and you're never going to get a better opportunity than this.

You unlock the door, push it open, and step inside — only to find yourself face to face with Detective Riordan himself.

"Well, well. Look who it is," Detective Riordan remarks.

Is he talking to you or is Detective Chan also in the apartment somewhere? It's your last coherent thought before the beige carpet heaves up to hit you in the face.

When you finally come around, you're lying flat on your back on Robert's none-too-clean floor and Detective Riordan is straddling you.

He seems to have ripped your shirt wide open and he's rubbing your chest with his big, powerful hands.

22

Suddenly life just got a lot more interesting —
especially when he leans forward and covers your mouth
with his own.

If you kiss Detective Riordan back,
turn to page 27

If sanity reasserts itself and you shove him off,
turn to page 43

If you decide to take another look at that picture
where you and Detective Riordan have sex,
turn to page 9

When you arrive at Café Noir, Claude ushers you to a booth in the back where you can close your eyes and relax for a few minutes. You listen to Piaf singing *"Non, je ne regrette rien,"* and you try not to think about what Robert's last moments must have been like. In fact, you try not to think about Robert at all because if you let yourself go down that path, it's going to be hard to find your way back.

It's funny how you can spend every day with someone and yet still be going in completely different directions.

Eventually Claude reappears and sets a plate of linguine before you. The sharp-sweet scent of garlic and basil wafts from the tangle of pasta. You're surprised to find that you actually are sort of hungry. He opens a bottle of wine, fills two glasses, and sits down across from you.

You don't want to ask, but you have to because even you can't help but notice Claude is acting a *little* suspiciously.

"So what really happened between you and Rob?" you ask.

Claude hedges, but what it comes down to is pretty much what you suspected: Claude and Robert had a little fling followed by a big bust up. Claude says the details are his business, and you agree. Except…

Except Claude wrote some, er, colorful letters and poems that he thinks may come back to bite him in the ass. In a manner of speaking.

24

"You could get those letters back, Adrien," he says to you. "Listen, petit, you're his best friend. Were. You're his boss. You could come up with a legitimate excuse for going over there."

"No. No. No," you say, showing exceptionally good judgment for once.

"I wouldn't ask if it wasn't —"

"Read my lips. *Non.*"

If you let your commonsense and instinct for self-preservation fall prey to emotional blackmail, turn to page 21

If you decide to resist that soft, pleading gaze of Claude's, put down your fork and turn to page 30

You work until about three o'clock and then you can't ignore your growling stomach any longer, so you head over to that burger chain you like so much — even though you know it's so bad for you.

You order a burger with bacon and cheese, french fries, and a giant Coke. Then you cancel the order for the Coke because you have plenty of Tab back at the bookstore and you prefer that anyway.

The kid in the brown and orange (what sadist came up with that uniform?!) pantsuit sighs heavily so that you fully understand what a total PIA you are because you Do This Every Time. You apologize guiltily, grab your lunch bag, and retreat back to your lair.

But as you let yourself in through the side door of the bookstore, you're startled and alarmed to hear what sounds like one of the bookshelves crashing over. It would take an earthquake to budge those things and as far as you can tell, the earth is steady beneath your feet. Okay, not totally steady, but that's because your legs are shaking.

Another shelf goes crashing over and the whole building shakes.

Your bewildered gaze takes in books thrown everywhere: dumped in the aisles, scattered across the polished wood floor. The mahogany counter is swept bare of everything except the computerized register, which is bolted down. The cash drawer is open and empty.

You've been robbed!

But since they've got the money, why are the bastards still here? Why didn't they take their ill-gotten gains and flee? Or are they venting their frustration with how measly the ill-gotten gains are by trashing your bookstore?

If you decide to confront the intruder on your own,
turn to page 14

If you decide to run next door to call the police,
turn to page 47

You open your mouth to that kiss and for a strange few seconds you share warm, moist breaths with Detective Riordan. His mouth is both firm and soft. He tastes...

Wow.

You are *kissing* Detective Riordan. And the weirdest part of all is he's a very good kisser. His lips press insistently against yours. He's totally getting into this.

He's not alone.

Osculate. Oscillate. What the hell is the word? Is there a word? Will you ever be able to form words again because this...is...so...crazy...

Crazy and sweet. So sweet.

He tastes like no one you've ever kissed before. Darker. Is dark a flavor?

You keep your lashes shut tight because you don't want to break the spell. Tentatively, as the kiss deepens, you touch the tip of your tongue to the tip of his tongue. His tongue flicks delicately against yours. You experience that contact as vividly as an electric shock — and that shock seems to snap Detective Riordan back to sanity.

He pulls back sharply, lifting off you. At the same instant, you're scrambling out from under him, sitting up, pushing your hair out of your eyes.

"What was that?" you demand, as if you didn't know perfectly well. You're not *that* out of practice.

28

Detective Riordan kneels in front of you, his face flushed, his eyes dark with emotion. He says defensively, "I thought you were having a heart attack."

"That is some bedside manner, I gotta say."

If possible, Detective Riordan goes still redder. "I thought you stopped breathing."

"I nearly did!"

He makes some noises about arresting you for breaking and entering, but he doesn't produce handcuffs. Then he informs you that Robert's apartment has already been searched, which is aggravating. Mostly because — as he does not fail to mention — you really should have thought of this yourself.

You tell him you didn't kill Robert. You can't tell if he believes you or not, but he suggests you go somewhere and talk about it.

If you decide to go with Detective Riordan,
turn to page 75

If you feel discretion is the better part of valor,
turn to page 45

"I'm trying to help you, Mr. English," Bruce Green says. "My informant tells me LAPD plans to make you the scapegoat for Hersey's murder.

"Your finger hovers over the disconnect button, but you wait. The fact is, you're starting to wonder the same thing."

You're gay and that's good enough for LAPD."

"I don't believe that," you reply. "Anyway, you're wasting your time. I don't know anything. I didn't kill Robert. That's the only thing I know."

"You'd better talk to somebody, Mr. English. Tell your story," advises Green. "Your next interview with Riordan and Chan will be downtown, take my word for it. They plan to have an arrest by the end of the week."

This is exactly what you're afraid of and you have to struggle to speak. "What is it you think you can do for me?"

"I can get the support of the gay community behind you. We'll put your story on the front page: the story of how LAPD is trying to railroad an innocent gay man because they're too prejudiced and lazy to do their job."

Oh God. Oh God. Oh God.

If you decide to hear what Bruce Green has to say,
turn to page 46

If you decide to hang up on him and hope for the best,
turn to page 25

You're still thinking over Claude's crazy request when you arrive back at Cloak and Dagger. As you unlock the side door and push it open, you realize at once that something is very wrong. Books are scattered everywhere, in fact, entire shelves have been knocked over. Chairs lie on their side. Even the framed prints on the wall have been torn down and smashed.

Just when you thought the day couldn't get any worse.

Numbly, you turn to the counter, and sure enough the cash register drawer is open and empty. Not that there is ever a lot of cash in there, but that's not the point. You find the phone behind the counter. It still works. You call 911. You've been taking it for granted the intruder got away, but now you wonder if you're being overly optimistic.

Maybe he's hiding in the back of the store. If you weren't so shocked and angry, you'd probably wait for the cops outside, but you are completely and uncharacteristically pissed off at this...this violation.

You grab the poker lying in front of the faux fireplace and you head for your office. What you find there leaves you feeling sick. It's one thing to steal, but why this wanton violence? Boxes of books have been tipped over and emptied. Desk drawers have been hauled out and dumped — same story with the file cabinet. Your heart pills are crushed and sprinkled throughout the papers like the dust you'll eventually be.

Jeez, that's a morbid thought. But this kind of thing would make anyone feel like there isn't much of a point.

At least the intruder is gone. He's not hiding in the back and he doesn't seem to have broken into your living quarters.

The skull sitting at the top of the stairs is a nice touch.

When the cops finally arrive — oh joy, Detectives Riordan and Chan again — you're sitting on the staircase trying not to have a heart attack. Literally.

Turn to page 39

If you want to sail ahead to the part where
the pirate ship appears on the horizon,
turn to page 32

"**B**ring the prisoner to my cabin," Captain English drawls, sliding his cutlass into its scabbard and absently straightening the snowy cuffs of his linen shirt.

(Psst! YOU'RE Captain English! Remember? Don't just stand there gaping. This isn't a movie.)

You saunter ahead of your men as they hustle the still struggling, big, blond, Royal Naval officer across the rolling deck and down a narrow stairway. The scent of timber and tar mingle with sweat and gunpowder. The ship murmurs to herself in anticipation. The battle has been fought, the spoils won.

You reach your cabin, throw open the door, and your prisoner is hurled inside your richly appointed quarters. Watery blue light filters through the three sides of massive windows, hundreds of glittering prisms created by diamond-shaped panes of glass. Your prisoner sprawls and lands face first on the sumptuous purple Persian carpet. The chart table is littered with rolled and unrolled maps, your compass, your spyglass. Carved and lacquered chests are brimming over with books, for when you're not marauding the high seas, you like to curl up with a good murder mystery.

You nod for your men to retreat. They hesitate, but you wave them off impatiently. In addition to your cutlass, you carry a pistol in the pocket of your greatcoat. You're not worried about whether you can handle one slightly-the-worse-for-wear salty sea dog.

The door closes quietly behind First Mate Angus Gordon. Your prisoner lies where he has fallen. You watch the slow, steady rise and fall of his broad, muscular back beneath the torn and blackened rags of his shirt. Under those dashingly tight black breeches, the man's arse is taut and perfectly formed. Hunger flicks to life inside you. If you're perfectly honest, that hunger never fully sleeps.

"Welllll, my treasure," you say in a voice that isn't quite as steady and hard as you might wish. "Would you like to tell me your name?"

Your prisoner raises his head. His hair is guinea gold, his eyes are the green gilt of ancient Venetian beads. "Lieutenant James Patrick Riordan," he rasps in a voice like rough velvet.

"Ah, Irish," you murmur. "I've no quarrel with the Irish."

"But I've a quarrel with you, Captain English. I'm a servant of Her Majesty the Queen," Riordan says.

He appears to be serious. His eyes glitter dangerously as they meet yours. Your smile widens.

"I see. Well, you know how this works. You can join up with me and my crew — if I may say, we *do* offer one of the finest benefit packages this side of the equator, including comprehensive health care and retirement plans — or I can slit your gullet here and now. Your choice."

"Feel free to try and slit my gullet," Riordan says and jackknifes into a fighting position.

Not again. Maybe it's your presentation? Maybe PowerPoint would help?

Riordan sidesteps and begins to circle you.

You sigh. He's a large man. Shoulders wide as a gangplank. Fit. *Very* fit. But as you've noted over the years, the bigger they are, the harder they fall. You drop to your haunches, and yank the carpet out from under his big flat feet.

Lieutenant Riordan crashes down just like the mast of his ship fell beneath your cannon ball. He conks his handsome golden head against the sturdy leg of your chart table and it's lights-out for all hands.

By the time your prisoner regains consciousness, you have him tied and spread-eagled on your big comfy pirate bed. He tugs experimentally at one of the silk scarves looped around the carved bedpost.

You finish lighting the lamps, undress, and join him in the soft cloud of plum lambs wool blankets and paisley satin sheets. Tiny flames dance in the frosted amber globes, casting warm shadows over his sleek, limber body.

"Don't even think about it," Riordan warns. His voice is low, fierce.

You stroke a delicate finger over the curve of his buttock, and he shivers. "But I have been thinking about it. I've been thinking about it ever since I saw you slit my midshipman's throat," you purr.

Riordan chokes out, "You seem to have an unseemly preoccupation with slits and slitting, Captain English."

A bubble of laughter rises in your throat. You swallow it. You haven't had such fun in a long while. "How very right you are, Lieutenant."

You pounce, covering his long, strong body with yours.

"Grrrrr." You nip the nape of his neck, and he starts. You kiss the bite mark, nuzzle him, nuzzle his ears, the side of his throat. He swallows hard. He smells of sweat and smoke and salt. He smells like a man.

You want this so much, more than you've wanted anything in a very long time. Your mouth is dry, your heart pounds violently, your cock is so stiff it hurts.

"I'll kill you," Lieutenant Riordan warns.

"It's worth it," you whisper and proceed to press a trail of kisses down his spine.

He stills. Indeed, he barely seems to breathe as you plant each teasing deliberate kiss all the way down to the damp velvet dip of tailbone.

"Shall I shiver your timbers, my treasure?" you ask. It never hurts to ask, after all.

Usually they say yes.

Uh oh.

It appears you have not been paying proper attention. Lieutenant Riordan must have worked one hand free and then untied his other wrist. He suddenly rolls over and now you are pinned beneath his larger and more powerful body. He chuckles evilly at your astonished chagrin, covering your mouth with his, swallowing your protests. It's that whole sweet savage possession thing you pirates are so fond of, and it leaves you feeling sort of hot and weak and shivery inside.

"How v-very d-dare you!" you stutter, when you have breath to speak again.

Riordan laughs.

You try to knee him in the guts, but maybe he went to the same prep school because that basically ends up with you making it easier for him to find the unguarded entrance to your body.

No, no, no. This can't be happening. But yes, the lieutenant's finger is up your arse.

His oil slick fingers move inside your body and now you are writhing, whimpering helplessly, begging him to do more, do whatever he wants to you.

"What, this?" he asks innocently, and presses the spongy little nub that makes you want to scream with pleasure. "Or maybe this?"

Tears spring to your eyes. It's so sweet. So good. You know you should be fighting him. Hells bells. You could summon assistance by simply raising your voice. You know

it, but somehow all you can do is nod and pant and nod again as he continues that leisurely teasing and tormenting.

"I'm going to do all that," he promises, his hot breath sending chills of sensation over your bare skin. "I'm going to do it to you all night long. But first, I want to hear you say the words."

"Wh-what words?" you moan.

"You know."

"P-P-please?"

"Warm."

"Pretty please?"

"Warmer."

Oh, and it *is* warmer. Deliciously, delectably hot. It's hard to think with his knowing fingers sending little flashes of dizzying delight through your trembling body. But gradually you understand what he wants, what has really happened here.

You swear softly. But there's no use pretending. You say huskily, "I surrender, Jamie."

James laughs softly and licks your ear. "Good. Me too, Captain English."

The End

It doesn't help — you absorb the fact with dismay — that they think you faked this burglary.

"They didn't break in." Riordan rejoins Chan at the foot of the stairs and they hold a brief undervoiced conference. Not so undervoiced that you can't hear them — and their suspicions.

"They must have used Robert's key," you tell them.

Riordan glances up at you. "Yeah, maybe."

"*Maybe?*" The irritating thing is, that even in this moment of stress, you just can't help noticing how unfairly attractive the asshole is. Long legs encased in Levi's, powerful shoulders straining the seams of a surprisingly well-cut tweed jacket…, he's not your type, but then you don't really have a type anymore.

Riordan asks for your keys in order to check out the upstairs and you can't think of a good reason to refuse. When he gets done stomping around overhead, he and Chan exchange some meaningful looks (not *that* kind of meaningful look because these two are strictly of the heterosexual variety) and they hold a little impromptu third degree.

"Well," Riordan drawls. "You didn't tell us everything this morning, did you?"

You knew this was coming sooner or later. You say feebly, "I'm not sure what you mean."

Riordan smiles. Lots of perfect white teeth. The better to eat you with. Better not to think about that.

Chan says, "We were just over at the Blue Parrot. We thought we'd clear up a couple of points with you."

"Such as why you lied," Riordan chimes in.

It goes downhill from there.

You admit to arguing with Robert over his repeated swiping of the petty cash, but you remind them that that would be a pretty lame motive for murder. Except, as Riordan points out, lots of people kill for lame reasons. MOST people kill for lame reasons.

That's probably true, but what they don't understand, probably can't understand, is that you loved Rob. Maybe you weren't crazy about who he grew up to be, but you still loved him. And you would do anything to take back that stupid argument.

Except you can't.

Riordan and Chan try to get you to admit you were sleeping with Robert, but you weren't. He never asked. And hopefully you'd have had the brains to turn him down if he had. Otherwise, these two might be legitimately questioning you right now.

You swallow hard and say as calmly and quietly as you can. "Robert left before I did last night. He left to meet someone. Didn't the bartender confirm that?"

Chan snaps his gum. "Sure did. Robert left at 6:45 and you stayed and had a second Midori margarita. You left at about 7:30. Fifteen minutes later, Robert showed up again looking for you."

Amazingly, the police do not arrest you and you are left to spend the rest of the evening thinking about all the things you should — would — do differently if you had a second chance. Unfortunately, your second chances don't begin until Rob is already dead, so you just have to keep turning pages and see if you can salvage something.

Why did Rob come back to the Blue Parrot? Did he feel as bad as you did about that final argument? Or was he still angry, still looking for a fight?

You're never going to know.

Later that night, Tara, Rob's wife — widow — phones.

"You killed him." Tara's voice is so low you can barely hear the words, and when you do understand them, your hair stands up like a porcupine's quills. Luckily, it's a good look on you.

"What are you talking about?"

"You killed him just as surely as if you'd stuck the knife in his chest."

Yeah, the conversation doesn't go so well. Tara is under the misapprehension that Rob left her in order to be with you. Whereas, in fact, Rob left her to be with everyone in L.A. Of course, you cannot say this. In fact, there's not much you can say except to swear up and down that you never regarded Rob as anything but a friend (which isn't technically true, but yet *is* true as far as it affected the outcome of Tara's marriage).

Tara concludes the evening's performance by wishing you a horrible death.

You finish up by getting drunk and watching an old pirate movie on TV.

Sadly, you don't have a lot of choices this evening. Sometimes it goes that way.

If you want to sail ahead to the part where
the pirate ship appears on the horizon,
turn to page 32

Or you can always turn to page 65

As Detective Riordan's firm, warm lips latch onto yours, you feel a surge of, well, hopefully alarm, though probably not.

You plant your hands on his pecs and give him a good, hard shove. He's not expecting it, and topples backwards.

"What the hell was *that?*" you demand. Apparently it's been a while.

"I thought you were having a heart attack." Riordan's face is flushed.

"Most people just call 911. Or were you kissing me in gratitude for removing myself from your investigation?"

Riordan glowers at you and then, unexpectedly, laughs. "You are kind of a nuisance," he agrees.

"What are you doing here?" you ask suspiciously.

"I think that's my line. What exactly were you searching for, English?"

You make up some bullshit about needing work papers that you think Robert might have accidentally taken home. Riordan hears you out with a sardonic expression. He waits until you've come to a complete and full stop.

"Uh huh. Did it not occur to you that we would have already conducted a search of the premises?"

Well, yes. But for some reason you were thinking the cops would maybe not know what to look for. Although

44

love — and hate — letters would hardly be something the police would overlook.

You must look suitably chagrined because Riordan gives another of those hard laughs. He suggests the two of you go somewhere so you can have a little chat. You're not sure if the invitation is optional or not.

If you decide to go with Detective Riordan,
turn to page 75

If you feel discretion is the better part of valor,
turn to page 45

You are preoccupied on the drive back to Pasadena, and no wonder. Riordan cannot be straight. No straight guy ever kissed another guy like that. Like he'd been waiting all his life to lock lips with his fellow man. Like you're the best thing he ever tasted, and he wanted to make a three-course meal of you.

You can't stop thinking about that kiss (or near kiss, if you're joining us from page 43 and every time you do let yourself think about it, you feel weak in the knees. So it's a good thing you're already sitting down.

After you merge onto the freeway, it occurs to you that you should call Claude and let him know what happened.

If you fish out your cell phone
and call Claude right now,
turn to page 71

If you wait to call Claude till you've arrived
at Cloak and Dagger books,
turn to page 149

Bruce suggests that you meet for a quick coffee down the street. The place just happens to be one of your favorites, and you agree. After the morning you've had, you could use a time out. You lock up the bookstore and walk down to the coffee house.

You're sitting on a stool, sipping your coffee and gazing out the plate glass window when you spot a tall, black-haired man in a dark suit, jogging across the street. The man neglects to look both ways and he's struck by a passing car. You watch in horror as he flies up and lands on the hood of the car, before tumbling lifelessly to the street.

Traffic comes to a screeching halt. People, yourself included, pour out of the shops and restaurants and gather around the scene of the accident to see what can be done.

Unfortunately, nothing can be done, and the man — who turns out to be Bruce Green, the reporter from *Boytimes* — dies right there in front of you.

Truly one of the very worst days of your life.

A week later Claude is arrested for Robert's murder. When you eventually learn about Claude's violent past, you're saddened but not surprised. As much as you loved Robert, he could have driven a saint to the breaking point.

The End

As quietly as possible you sneak back out of the bookstore and run like hell to the Thai restaurant next door, slipping in through the open kitchen door. Frantically, you try to explain your situation to the astonished cooks.

It takes a minute or two, but once your neighbors understand your plight, they grab an assortment of meat cleavers and butcher knives and race over to the bookstore just in time to confront a tall, rawboned man in black jeans and a black turtleneck. The man has lank, dark hair, brown eyes, and a gaunt face that you're sure you've never seen before.

He stares at you for a long, strange moment and begins to cry.

Do you know him?

The intruder tries to run, but your neighbors are in no mood for fooling around. They surround him, threateningly waving their weapons. The police are summoned and Detectives Riordan and Chan arrive right after the uniforms.

The intruder breaks down and confesses he is a former schoolmate of yours, Grant Landis. The name doesn't ring a bell.

Landis claims he killed Robert to avenge some perceived slight back in high school. You're really having trouble following his story, but it seems like maybe it had something to do with the Chess Club.

Landis is still babbling when he's hustled into the black and white police cruiser and taken away.

Detective Riordan approaches you and brusquely apologizes for giving you a hard time that morning. You get the feeling he wants to say more, but what is there to say?

Apology over, he says curtly, "Take care, Mr. English."

You nod stiffly.

Riordan hesitates, then slips on his reflector shades. He looks cool and impassive as he studies you. Then he turns and walks away.

The End

Green suggests you go somewhere and get a drink together. That sounds good to you. You could use a drink after the funeral service.

You follow him to a little pub in Atwater Village called The Griffin. It's a little brick box with red, black and white striped awnings. Inside it's dark and empty. The Beatles play on the jukebox, which is generally a good sign. You're not really paying attention though, your thoughts still back with Messrs. Riordan and Chan. Do they really think you killed Robert for his insurance money? It's a surprise to you that Robert even bothered with insurance. That would have to have been Tara's doing because Robert never thought a week ahead.

You wonder why Claude did not come to Robert's funeral. But then again, maybe he stayed away because he's hoping the police don't know about him yet.

Call-Me-Bruce gets the first round. While he's at the bar, you use the men's room. When you return to the table, Bruce is munching morosely on a handful of peanuts. He smiles at you, and his face changes. He's more attractive than you realized. Or maybe the drinks are stronger here.

Actually, they are pretty strong. You feel the whisky and soda almost at once. You should have made time for breakfast.

"The smartest thing you can do," Bruce is saying earnestly, "is put yourself completely in my hands. I'll get your story out there. I'll make sure you have the full support of the gay community behind you."

You know he means well, but there are few issues that attract the full support of ANY community, and you find it hard to believe that anyone is going to rally around you without more evidence that you didn't have anything to do with Robert's death. After all, there is a fair bit of circumstantial evidence against you. In recent times, you and Robert had a rocky relationship, you argued in public the night he was murdered, and you were one of the last people to see him alive.

Of course you had no motive to kill Robert, but motive means a lot more to you than it does to the police.

"I don't really have a story," you tell Bruce. "There really isn't anything to tell."

He smiles in polite disbelief. "You and Hersey were lovers, weren't you?

"You choke on your drink. "Rob and *me*? No way."

"Really? It seems to me like he must have had feelings for you."

"Why would you say that?"

"Just little hints I've picked up."

"Like what?" you insist.

Bruce smiles regretfully. "I can't reveal my source."

Who has he been talking to? Someone who doesn't have a clue, obviously. Or maybe someone who wants to get you in trouble with the police? You say, "Your source has it wrong. Robert and I were friends from way back, but the way back is all we really had in common."

He studies you thoughtfully. "If you say so."

"I do say so."

"In that case, what's your opinion as to why the police are so sure you killed Robert?"

"According to the police, I'm just one of a number of suspects."

"You don't really believe that, do you? They're going to arrest you. I guarantee it."

He seems so completely sure of his facts. It's unsettling. Disturbing. If only you could think more clearly, but that drink has really gone to your head. You feel almost woozy.

"Another?" Bruce asks, rising. He's smiling at you.

"No. Thanks..." You should probably get this round, but the fact is, you're not sure you can stand up.

All at once you're drunk off your ass. Or on your ass. Yes, that's it. You're drunk on your ass. You smother a laugh.

Bruce moves off to the bar and you blearily puzzle over your predicament. You actually have a pretty good head for alcohol. True, you didn't eat and you're not sleeping well and it's been an emotionally exhausting day, but...

Bruce finally comes back and places another drink in front of you. He sips his own and begins talking again, but you don't hear a word of it. His voice sounds far away and echo-y.

Finally you feel obliged to interrupt. It's either that or put your head down on the table and go to sleep. "Bruce, I'm sorry. I'm not feeling very well."

His brows draw together. "What's the matter, Adrien?"

"I'm just...I need to go home." How are you going to get home? You can't drive like this. You're not even sure you can walk. You're going to have to call a cab. You should surely be able to manage that, right? Just find your phone and...fuck...you've dropped your phone and if you bend down, you're liable to wind up face first on the floor...

Oh. But it's okay because Bruce is coming around to help you. He retrieves your phone, pockets it, helps you to your feet. He's stronger than he looks. He gets you on your feet and walks you out to your car. He helps you into the passenger seat and gets behind the wheel.

"Just relax, Adrien," he tells you. "You're okay now. I'm going to take good care of you."

That's the last thing you remember until he's helping you out of the car again. You're back at Cloak and Dagger, and Bruce is walking you through the towering maze of bookshelves and up the mountain of stairs. You look over the railing and down at Angus who gazes silently up, his glasses glinting like two enormous sunspots. He's saying something, and Bruce answers, but the words sound fuzzy and foreign.

The next time you open your eyes, it's eight o'clock at night. You're in bed, nude, and you're pretty sure that you've been drugged. Drugged and maybe worse. You're not sure because you're feeling pretty stiff and achy, and you seem to have picked up a few bruises in places you don't typically bruise.

The last thing you remember was having a drink with Bruce Green at a bar in Atwater Village.

Is it possible Bruce drugged you?

No. No, that's ridiculous.

But as you slowly move around your living quarters, you see little signs of disturbance. Drawers not quite flush, cupboard doors ajar, items moved. Nothing dramatic, but you live on your own and you're pretty set in your various routines. You notice when things are different...and this evening everything is different.

You sit down on the sofa, feeling confused and shaky. None of this makes sense.

Or does it? Bruce is a reporter after all. Maybe he took advantage of your drinking too much to snoop around your place.

But that's the problem. You *didn't* drink too much. You had one drink. Even taking into account skipping breakfast and not sleeping well, one drink should not have knocked you out for most of the afternoon.

You can't find your phone either. Or your keys.

You're in the midst of a panicked search when you hear the downstairs buzzer. Someone is knock-knock-knocking on your wee cottage door. What the hell now?

You stumble downstairs and who should be leaning on your buzzer but granite-faced Detective Riordan.

"Where have you been all day?" he demands. "I've left you three messages."

"I-I've been out." Which is true.

"Listen, English. I get that your mother is a big society dame, but you don't get to ignore phone calls from the police. I can make your life very uncomfortable — and that's whether you actually killed your pal Hersey or not. Understand?"

So here's a weird thing. You don't particularly like Detective Riordan. In fact, he makes you nervous. *And* he thinks you're a murderer. But as you stare into his narrowed, suspicious hazel eyes, something seems to shift inside your chest. You're relieved to see him. You don't even mind him yelling at you.

You open your mouth to explain yourself, but you don't know where to begin. So you stand there making like a guppy. But then something *is* fishy, right?

Maybe Riordan is a decent detective after all, because he seems to correctly interpret your appalled expression and inability to speak.

"What's wrong with you? Has something happened?" His voice is still hard, but you hear a note of something...

concern? Kindness? Probably whatever it was that first made him want to become a cop.

"I'm not even sure," you answer. And then you have to stop because your throat closes as tight as if someone tried to throttle you.

Riordan studies you, frowning, and then he says calmly, "Why don't we go inside and talk about it?"

It's a relief to have even so small a plan of action. You lead the way upstairs. You offer Riordan a drink. He tells you to sit down and then he makes coffee. He seems perfectly at ease moving around your kitchen, finding mugs, spoons, cream, sugar. He puts what tastes like a cup of sugar in yours, and you realize that he thinks you're in shock. And that he's right.

You drink the coffee and you do feel better. You tell Riordan the whole story. He listens without interrupting. But then it's not a long or complicated story.

"I know it's ridiculous," you finish up. "But..."

"You think you've been raped?" Riordan asks quietly.

Hearing it put so baldly makes you feel very weird, almost lightheaded. What seemed like maybe one of the least important aspects of all this is the first thing Riordan has glommed onto. You wish he wouldn't, because you don't want to think about that possibility.

It's hard even to say this much. "I don't know."

"There's one way to find out."

"I don't think I can —"

"You need to find out." He says it with brusque kindness. "You'll want to get tested. You'll *need* to get tested."

"Yes. I understand. I will. But I can't..." You take a deep breath. "I'm sorry, because I know it's going to sound chickenshit, but even if it's true, even if this is some kind of date rape, I can't press charges. I can't go to court over something like this. I just...can't."

Riordan is silent. He says at last, "Then I don't know what you think I can do for you."

You stare at him and you can see that he is angry. Not with you. He's frustrated with you but he's angry on your behalf. He genuinely cares about this. It eases something inside you.

You smile. "I don't think you can do anything for me," you admit. "I just had to talk to someone. So thank you. You already have helped."

Now it's his turn to stare. His face flushes and he says in an odd voice, "No. Hell no. He's not getting away with this."

"I don't —"

"I am. Are you sure you were drugged?"

Yeah. You're sure about that. There's a weird aftertaste in your mouth and you feel sick and shaky in a way that alcohol has never affected you. "I'm sure he drugged me. I'm sure he searched my place. And if he doesn't have my phone and my keys, I sure as hell don't know where they are."

Riordan is silent. At last he gets to his feet. "Okay. Leave this to me."

What does that mean? You have no idea, but you accompany Riordan downstairs. He pauses just outside the front door. "If Green's got your keys, don't stay here tonight," he says. "Do you have some place you can spend the night?"

You could go to Claude's. You could go to your mother's. You have a number of friends who could put you up for the night. You don't feel like going anywhere, but you nod.

"I'll be in touch," Riordan says, and he vanishes into the smog-scented night.

You go back upstairs and phone a taxi. You throw a couple of things in a bag. It'll be easier to go to a hotel than try to explain to a friend, let alone your mother, why you need shelter for the night. Plus...you don't want to talk. You don't want to think. You don't even want to drink. You want to hole up someplace warm and quiet. And secure. Some place with deadbolts and maybe a security guard. Or two.

You go downstairs and double check that Angus has locked everything up. You find your keys and your cell phone on the desk in your office where apparently Bruce left them for you.

It's a jolt. If you're wrong about Bruce walking off with your keys and phone, what else did you get wrong? Maybe everything. Maybe you did just have too much to drink? Maybe you just sicced Detective Riordan on the guy who was kind enough to see you safely home after you got drunk and passed out after Robert's funeral.

Oh hell.

You're still working this out when you hear a key in the side door lock.

You walk out of the office in time to see Bruce coming in the side door carrying a couple of bags of groceries.

"Oh good, you're awake," he says. He puts the groceries on the wooden counter and comes around to kiss you. "How are you feeling? Pretty hung over, I guess?"

"What are you doing here?" You gesture to the sacks of groceries. "What's all this?"

"Solid food." He adds teasingly, "We don't all like to drink our meals."

"What's that supposed to mean?" Any of it. All of it. What is going on? "Why are you here?"

"That's exactly what I was going to ask," a new voice puts in. Detective Riordan is standing in the doorway.

Bruce looks in confusion to Riordan and then you. "You asked me to move in," he says.

"Huh?"

"This afternoon." Bruce smiles self-consciously. "After we…" Bruce's smile fades. "Are you saying you don't remember?"

"There's no way." You're talking to Riordan. "No way in hell."

Riordan's face doesn't give anything away. Maybe he believes you, maybe he doesn't. Bruce's confusion and hurt seem pretty believable too, even you can see that.

Riordan asks for Bruce's version of the afternoon's events and the long and short of it is, Bruce interviewed you after Robert's funeral, you got wasted, and Bruce saw you home like the gentleman he is. You begged him to stay with you, begged him to fuck you, then afterwards you passed out, and somewhere in the middle of all that Bruce fell for you because, wow, who wouldn't be charmed by a promiscuous alcoholic subject to blackouts? Okay, Bruce doesn't quite put it like that, in fact he's very tactful in his recital (because you're his new boyfriend, after all), but he does hint that he knew from interviewing your friends that you've got major issues as well as a drinking problem. He just didn't realize how serious your situation was until this very minute when you've rejected him after your afternoon of mad passion.

He seems more sad than angry as Riordan escorts him from the premises.

When Riordan finally returns, you say, "I don't care what his story is. I had one drink. And even if I had ten drinks, I wouldn't ask anyone to move in with me. *Ever.*"

Riordan blinks at the vehemence of that. "Okay."

"You've been investigating me too. Do any of my friends say I'm a drunk?"

"No."

"Do they say I've got major issues?"

"Well —"

"Funny. Look, maybe I did ask him to drive me home, but I didn't ask him to stay. I know me. I wouldn't."

Riordan asks, "Did he leave the keys and your phone on your office desk?"

"Yes. But he also had a key made! You saw that, right? He just let himself in here."

"Well, he thought he was moving in."

You have no answer to that.

Riordan says, "Look, I don't know what's going on, but there's a taxi outside waiting for you. I think maybe you'd be smart to stay somewhere else tonight."

You nod. "I will."

"I'll be in touch."

You spend the night at a hotel and the next day you have all the locks in the bookstore changed again, inside and out. Bruce phones you a couple of times, but you don't pick up. After that, you don't hear from Bruce and you don't hear from Riordan.

Two uncomfortable days pass. You don't hear from the cops at all — not even about the murder investigation.

Then, three days after the funeral, Detective Riordan shows up at the bookstore at closing time.

"Let's go upstairs," he says curtly. "You're going to need a drink." Before you can get too indignant, he adds, "*I* need a drink."

You lead the way upstairs and ask Riordan what he'd like to drink. He was apparently serious about needing one because he asks for whiskey, if you've got it. You pour him two fingers of Bushmills.

"You'd better pour yourself one."

His expression is so bleak, you obey.

"Cheers," he says, and touches his glass to yours.

"Cheers."

"We arrested Bruce Green for Robert Hersey's murder this morning."

You choke on your whiskey, but manage to get it down without spewing. "Are you serious?" you rasp.

"I'm serious. I got curious about Green after the incident with you. I started checking around. A couple of Hersey's neighbors identified Green as the man Hersey was dating before his death. Also, I looked into Green's background and it turns out Bruce Green doesn't exist. Bruce Green was just an alias for a guy named Grant Landis. Does that name mean anything to you?"

"No. Should it?"

"Yeah. You went to high school with Landis. Apparently he had quite a crush on you."

"I don't remember anybody named Grant Landis."

"Well, he sure remembered you. His basement was plastered with pictures of you, starting with you at age sixteen in your tennis whites and ending with you sacked out and naked in your bedroom a couple of days ago."

You stare at Riordan. Heat floods your entire body and then drains away leaving you ice cold. You try to hide the fact that you're shaking by drinking more whiskey.

Riordan goes on to explain that Grant Landis has been knocking off your old high school classmates due to some scandal that happened while you were out sick during your junior year. You only follow about a third of the explanation because you can't get past the horror of realizing Bruce — Grant — killed Robert. Grant was here in your home. He could have killed you. You have no idea, in fact, what he did actually do to you — but maybe that's as well.

"Are you all right?" Riordan asks suddenly.

You nod. You have no idea if you're all right or not.

Riordan says he has to get back to the station, they're still processing Green — Landis — completing the slam dunk case against him.

You walk him to the door. "Thank you."

He seems to hesitate. "Will you be okay?"

"Yeah."

He doesn't move. You stare into his eyes and it occurs to you that if he wasn't straight you'd think that maybe he was...well...interested.

But he is straight, right?

"Good night," he says finally.

"Good night. And thank you again for believing me."

He nods, but...is that a flicker of disappointment in his gaze? If he leaves now, you probably won't see him again. Or at least, you won't get this chance again.

"Detective," you say quickly, as he turns away.

Riordan glances back.

"I was just wondering...you know how I write murder mysteries?"

He nods, looking slightly pained.

"Well, the thing is, I don't have any kind of background or resource for police procedure."

"I'll say," he says, abruptly energized. "I talked to your publisher, got a good look over that manuscript of yours." He shakes his head. "Christ. Where do you come up with this stuff?"

You ignore that, forging stubbornly on. "And I was wondering if, seeing that you are an expert, I could maybe...I don't know. Maybe call you sometime and, er, interview you?"

His expression lightens. "Yeah. Sure."

"We could get together and talk. Or maybe I could take you to dinner in payment. Or something. I don't know."

He looks thoughtful. He's not smiling exactly, but he does look sort of pleased. Cautiously pleased. "Yeah. Give me a call. I'll be happy to set you straight."

"Oh, I don't know if I want *that* exactly," pops out of your mouth.

He gives you a long look. He grins. "Call me Jake," he says.

The End

It rains the next morning. The rain drums down on the roof and beats against the windows. The narrow, one-way streets flood, as per usual, and customers are few and far between, which is fine, given the state of the bookstore after yesterday's break-in.

Your neighbors at the Thai restaurant helped you raise the fallen bookshelves, and you managed to carry out most of the broken glass, smashed bric-a-brac, and ruined books last night, but you can't help but feel depressed and worried.

Regardless of what the police think, you know that burglary was no coincidence.

But what could the burglar have been looking for? You remember the strange behavior of the tour group members — okay, the stranger than usual behavior of the tour group members. The lady with the frizzy dark hair and that old guy. What was his name? Henry Harrison. Could there be some connection between their wandering around your private rooms and the break-in? Could there be some connection to Rob's death?

It seems so unlikely. But more unlikely than Rob being murdered?

Your gloomy thoughts are interrupted by the arrival of Angus Gordon, a temp sent over by the employment agency. Angus is slim and slight, with John Lennon specs and a wispy goatee. He tells you he likes to be called "Gus," but you can't imagine anyone calls him Gus. You can't imagine anyone calls him much of anything.

You put him to work reshelving books.

A locksmith arrives before lunch to change all the locks, inside and out. The police did reluctantly admit that they did not find any keys on Rob's body or in his home, but you suspect they think you carried the keys off yourself after committing murder.

As hard as it is to believe, the police really do seem to believe you're a killer — and it's pretty clear to you that they are going to do their best to find enough evidence to build their case and arrest you.

After Angus leaves for lunch, the reporter from *Boytimes* phones again.

"You'd better talk to somebody, Mr. English. Tell your story," advises Bruce Green. "Your next interview with Riordan and Chan will be downtown, take my word for it. They plan to have an arrest by the end of the week."

You try to speak calmly, but with every word he's confirming your own fears.

"What is it you think you can do for me?"

"I can get the support of the gay community behind you. Just talk to me, Mr. English. Five minutes. That's all. Off the record."

If you decide to continue speaking to Bruce Green,
turn to page 46

If you decide to keep your own counsel,
turn to page 68

OR maybe you'd like another look at those pirates,
in which case turn to page 37

"Thank you, Mr. Green, but no thank you." You disconnect and go fix yourself Cup-a-Soup for lunch.

You spend the rest of the day sorting through the dumped papers and files, and worrying about being arrested. But maybe being arrested would be preferable to...well, other things.

What those other things might be, you don't quite dare think about.

That evening the Partners in Crime weekly writing group meets at the bookstore. Claude arrives first and again tries to persuade you to break into Robert's apartment and search for anything that might implicate him in the murder.

You point out that you're as much a suspect as he is — and if you are caught breaking into Robert's home you will definitely jump the queue to Suspect #1.

Does Claude realize how guilty he's acting?

Next, Ted and Jean Finch arrive. They offer the theory that Robert fell victim to a serial killer preying on the gay community.

You understand that they're trying to be helpful, but...really, no. Not. Helping.

The other two members of the group arrive. You remember that Max Siddons had some kind of run-in with Robert, though you don't remember the details.

Robert had his good qualities — and that's what you would like to focus on now — but you can't help noticing that not many people are grieving for him. It would be horrible to find out Robert was killed by a mutual friend. Or even a mutual acquaintance.

The rest of the week passes and before you know it, it's Friday and you're dusting off your Hugo Boss suit to wear to Robert's funeral.

It's not a big funeral, but both the police and the media show up. On your way to the gravesite, Tara confronts you. She apologizes for her hysterical phone call earlier in the week. You tell her it's okay. You understand. And in a way, you do.

No sooner do you leave Tara cleaning divots of grass and mud from her heels than you bump into a tall, rather homely man in an expensive suit.

He introduces himself as Bruce Green, the reporter who keeps calling you.

Green has warm, kind brown eyes and an attractive smile. You realize maybe you've been too hasty brushing him off.

While you're chatting with Green, trying to make up your mind about talking to him, Detectives Riordan and

70

Chan show up and ask to speak to you privately. That's one thing you know for sure you don't want to do.

If you decide to continue speaking to Bruce Green,
turn to page 49

If you decide to break into Robert's apartment,
turn to page 81

Despite the fact that you're traveling at about seventy miles an hour on a crowded freeway, you start fishing around for your cell phone. I guess you figure Claude can't wait to hear the news that the police already searched Robert's?

Anyway, you finally find your phone. You glance away from the road just long enough to find Claude's name in your "favorites," but traffic is an unpredictable thing. The semi truck in front of you comes to a sudden halt. You look up in time to see the hood of your Bronco plow right into his brake lights.

Thankfully you don't remember anything after that.

When you finally wake up in the hospital, you can't move your legs. Or your arms. Or anything from the neck down. Your doctor regretfully informs you that you've suffered a C4 spinal cord injury and you're lucky to be breathing on your own. And breathing is all you can do on your own. You're completely paralyzed. It's not even easy to speak up now when you need help. And you need help with everything. You can't scratch your nose, let alone pick up a glass of water or push off the blankets when you're too warm.

You're rarely too warm, though. Mostly you're cold. Cold and numb.

So you've gone from being a guy with a bad heart to a quadriplegic guy with a bad heart.

Not too long after the accident you have surgery and your spine is fused so that at least you will be able to sit erect in a wheelchair and not have to lie inert in bed all the time. No, now you can sit inert in your chair.

When you're well enough for visitors, Detective Riordan comes to see you. He brings flowers, and seems self-conscious about it. He tells you the investigation into Robert's death has moved in a different direction. The police are now looking into Tara's financial situation. She was seriously in debt so being the beneficiary of Robert's life insurance policy was a lifesaver for her. And of course she was a woman scorned, and everyone knows how that goes.

Detective Riordan clearly has you confused with someone who gives a damn. In case he hasn't noticed, you've got your own problems now. You let him know this in words of one syllable, and he goes away.

You spend a month in the ICU and then a couple of months in a very expensive rehabilitation center learning how to breathe properly and swallow so you won't strangle yourself.

It could be worse — as people can't seem to resist telling you. You could be dead. You hear that a lot. You're too polite to respond with what you're actually thinking. You are lucky in that your family is very wealthy and you'll have all the care you need, and since you require twenty-four-hour complete assistance with everything from bathing to eating, that's a very good thing.

While you're in rehab, you learn that your mother assumes you will move in with her after you're released. She's already handled the sale of Cloak and Dagger Books and had your belongings moved to her home in Porter Ranch. The house is being remodeled to accommodate the new and unimproved you, and she's busily interviewing private nurses.

Your options for suicide are reduced these days, but you can't help thinking a lot about driving your motorized wheelchair into oncoming traffic. If only your keepers will ever let you get near traffic again.

But then Claude comes to visit and suggests you move in with him. He confesses he's always been a little in love with you, and he wants to take care of you. "Someone has to, *ma belle.*"

Tears well in your eyes when Claude says you could be his partner in the restaurant. There's nothing wrong with your brain, and you've always been pretty good at business.

"We would make a good team, *non?*"

Hell. You can't wipe your eyes, you can't wipe your nose, crying is liable to drown you. The tears tickle their way down your face and you gulp in shuddery breaths. Claude makes a soothing sound, mops your wet face for you, holds a tissue for you to blow your nose. Welcome to the rest of your life.

74

As grateful as you are, you feel you have to be honest with Claude, and you tell him you've never thought of him as anything but a friend. A dear friend, but...a friend.

Claude just chuckles in that deep, sexy voice. He tells you love will come.

Which brings up another, though related, subject. But Claude just brushes off your concerns and repeats that love will come.

If you decide to move in with your mother,
turn to page 103

If you decide to move in with Claude,
turn to page 5

You go to Brits Restaurant and Pub on East Colorado Boulevard. There's a dining room, but you sit in the pub section which has a ten-seat bar — nine seats of which are empty — a small TV playing soccer, and a handful of uncomfortable little tables.

You order a Harp. Riordan orders a Bass ale.

"So what piece of incriminating evidence do you think you left at Hersey's?" Riordan inquires. He takes a long pull on his ale.

Drinking on duty. Hm. He didn't strike you as the type. But then you probably don't look like an amateur burglar either.

"I told you. I thought Robert might have brought some invoices home with him."

Riordan looks pained. "Come off it. You're smart. Sort of. You know how it works. You know there are channels. Not to mention the fact that Hersey would no more have brought his work home with him than he'd have tried out for Father of the Year."

"Well, let me ask you something," you say. "Why were you hanging out at Robert's apartment? What were *you* looking for?"

His eyes narrow, but he says mildly enough, "I was playing a hunch."

"What hunch?"

"That the murderer would return to the scene of the crime."

You suck in a sharp breath, but as you stare at him you realize that there is a gleam of humor in his hazel eyes.

"I didn't kill Robert. I'm not saying our friendship was what it used to be, but I didn't have any reason to want him dead. I *don't* want him dead." For some reason, you get a little choked up, so you reach for your beer.

Riordan watches you consideringly. "You took a big chance going over to his place. If it had been Chan or anyone else who caught you, you'd be on your way downtown right now."

"Why aren't I?"

Just for an instant his gaze wavers. He shrugs. "I don't think you killed Hersey. Not that I couldn't be wrong."

"You're not wrong. I didn't kill him. I couldn't kill anyone."

"Sure you could." Now his gaze is very direct. "Anyone is capable of killing under the right circumstances. That said, I think killing would be a last resort for your type."

"My...type?"

You figure he means gay, but he says, "Intelligent, sensitive, civilized."

It's an observation, not a compliment, but you flush anyway.

He adds, "But B&E is out of character for you too, so I could be wrong about you in other ways. If you didn't go back to Hersey's to cover your own tracks, then you're trying to protect someone else. Who?"

"No one."

"Who?"

"I told you why I went there."

"There are no secrets in a murder investigation, Adrien-with-an-e."

"I bet that's not true."

He says quietly, "It would be safer for you not to keep any secrets from me."

"What does that mean?"

"Exactly what I said. Trust me on this."

You say lightly, "Sadly, I have trust issues."

"Does this have something to do with Mel Davis?"

Somehow it's a shock to hear Mel's name in this context, and you must not be hiding that shock very well. Riordan grimaces. "Like I said, there are no secrets in a murder investigation. Is Davis the reason you have trust issues?"

You take a mouthful of beer, swallow, and admit finally, "Could be."

He waits for you to say more, but what is there to say? He's already seen first hand that you're not exactly built for endurance, no need to emphasize that you've been returned for a refund once already. But then you remember Riordan's efforts at resuscitation, and you feel warm and almost…silly. Yes. You feel silly because anything else would be…even sillier.

Riordan says, "See, if you can't trust me, I can't trust you either."

"Trust me with what?"

He shrugs. He drains his beer, looks at his watch and says, "I've got to get going. Watch your back, English."

Turn to page 149

All this time, the machinery has been humming, and now the humming changes its note to a shrill whistle. Sir Basil goes to the eye-piece and looks into it. Opening a door in the machinery, he disappears inside. He comes out soon, flushed and evidently elated.

"Bring the stretcher, English," he orders.

You bring the stretcher, placing it close to the machine. Then Sir Basil opens a metal door and gently eases out a human body.

It's Jake Riordan, unconscious but alive and breathing. You help the scientist to get Jake on the stretcher, noticing that his crushed legs are perfectly healed.

Together you carry the insensible man to a long seat. Jake's eyes are still closed, but his even breathing indicates that he is only sleeping.

Suddenly you point a finger and cry out. "My God, Sir Basil, look at his hands and feet!"

Jake Riordan, still lying like a recumbent bronze statue sculptured by a master, is perfect from shoulder to wrist, from thigh to ankle. But, somewhere in that diabolical machine through which he had passed, his hands and feet have undergone a hideous metamorphism which has transformed them from the well-formed extremities of a splendid young hunk into the hairy paws of a giant rat!

HUH?

80

How did you get over here?!

If I were you, English, I'd get back to the main storyline before Riordan wakes up.

Robert's apartment is not sealed. No official yellow tape stretches across the front door proclaiming it a crime scene. So...you have a key and a standing invitation. That counts for something right?

You unlock the door and let yourself inside. In the gloom, you can just make out the shapes of furniture and exercise equipment. You don't want to risk turning on the lights, so you use your pencil flashlight as you quickly go through Robert's few belongings. What conclusions can you draw from piles of bills and photos of the life Robert left behind? Not many. Robert kept a couple of his high school yearbooks and he kept Claude's letters and poems. *Sacre bleu!* Those poems!

Suddenly you hear the scrape of a key in the front door lock. You jam the lid on the box of poems and letters and leap into the closet, pulling it closed.

Through the plywood, you hear the front door open and then shut. A band of light appears beneath the bottom of the closet door. Your scalp prickles in horror.

A floorboard creaks.

Is Robert's murderer prowling through the apartment at this very moment?

You wait, drenched in sweat, your heart ready to explode from nerves and tension. Then the floor creaks again. The band of light beneath the door vanishes. The front door closes as quietly as it opened. You hear the snick of the lock.

Silence.

You open the closet and step out.

The overhead light switches on again. Detective Riordan leans against the front door, one hand resting casually on his jacket lapel, shoulder holster within easy reach.

He drawls, "That's one of the oldest tricks in the world, Adrien-with-an-e."

The next time you open your eyes, Detective Riordan is leaning over you, patting your cheek. He looks relieved as you blink up at him, though his face is instantly impassive again.He says, "You know, English, maybe you should consider another line of work. I don't think you're cut out for burglary."

No kidding. But instead you flutter your eyelashes and do your best to look meek and non-threatening. He takes your wrist in his warm, big grip, checking your pulse rate, so he probably knows you're not as helpless as you're trying to pretend. But when you fumble around for your pills and request a glass of water, he acquiesces.You actually do need a pill, which is irritating, but in a couple of minutes you're back to your normal self, such as it is. What's interesting is that, as you watch Riordan watching *you*, it occurs to you that...

Well, no. That can't be right.

But if he wasn't straight, that particular look would indicate...

Something.

Interest?

Or maybe just suspicion. He's definitely suspicious of you. It might be the Breaking and Entering thing.

Riordan informs you that Robert's apartment has already been searched, top to bottom. When he slowly says the words "top to bottom," he gives you a very direct look and you feel your face warming.

What the heck?

You tell him you didn't kill Robert. You can't tell if he believes you or not, but he suggests you go somewhere and talk about it.

If you decide to go with Detective Riordan,
turn to page 84

If you decide to go home instead — oh come on!
Who are you kidding?
Turn the damn page to 84

You take Riordan to Café Noir so that you can warn Claude that the cops are on the verge of discovering his identity. You know Riordan is eventually going to ask if you know who "Black Beauty" is, and you won't be able to lie without putting yourself in worse jeopardy than you're already in.

Claude is, naturally, not thrilled with you, but you've got bigger concerns. Detective Riordan shows you a white plastic chess piece. A queen.

"A piece exactly like this was found on Hersey's body."

"On his body?" you repeat uncertainly.

"Clutched in his hand." Riordan gives you a strange, unpleasant smile. "As Hersey lay dying, his assailant pressed this into his hand and folded his fingers around it. Held it closed. There were bruises on Hersey's hand."

"Fingerprints?"

"No fingerprints."

You swallow. It's more of a gulp. Riordan pockets the game piece. "Keep that to yourself. We haven't released it to the press yet."

"Why tell me?"

"Because I think you know what this chess piece means."

You don't. In fact, you're more confused than ever, but Riordan is clearly one of those guys who doesn't like to second guess himself. He's either sure you're guilty of Robert's murder and he's setting a trap for you, or he's going to use you to set a trap for someone else.

The next day is the first Saturday of the month, which is when you get together with your mother for brunch at the ancestral home in Porter Ranch.

If you choose to get together
for brunch with Lisa as usual,
turn to page 91

If you decide to hire a private detective
to help you clear your name,
turn to page 86

The PI's name is Gavin Spade.

He's got an upscale office in Old Town with retro décor and Spade Investigations stenciled on the door. All that's missing is a Girl Friday named Effie. You appreciate the attention to detail. You just hope Spade is more than the sum of his shticks.

Spade's handshake lasts maybe a second or two too long, and you give him a closer look. Nice. Very nice. Dark curly hair, long-lashed brown eyes, and a jaw like Dick Tracy.

He ushers you into his inner office, and waves you into a chair. He takes the chair behind the desk.

You explain your dilemma and he hears you out in grave, attentive silence.

When you at long last roll to a stop, Spade says, "So let me get this straight, Adrien — may I call you Adrien?"

You nod, clear your throat. "Yeah. Of course."

"You can call me Gavin, by the way."

"Okay, Gavin."

Gavin treats you to a dazzling smile. "I think you're very wise to tackle this thing head on, Adrien. I've got the greatest respect for the police, but I can tell you from long experience, their modus operandi is to grab the first and easiest solution and keep working it till they can make it fit."

You don't get told you're "very wise" a lot and you smile weakly in return.

"I'm working a couple of cases right now," Gavin admits. "But I'm going to make you — your case — a priority."

Flattering but potentially expensive, and you're a little short of cash these days. You say, "Okay. But maybe we should discuss your fee?"

"I'll work with your budget, don't worry about that, Adrien."

Every time Gavin says your name, says *Adrien*, in that slow, almost savoring way, you get this funny little fluttering sensation in your chest. Well, let's face it, you write mysteries and this guy is the living embodiment of every PI fantasy you ever had. Not that you realized you even had PI fantasies until this moment. But then you didn't realize you had cop fantasies either until —

The outer door to Gavin's office flies open and who should barge in but Detective Riordan. Speak of the Devil. His face is flushed and his blond hair looks ruffled. Or at least as ruffled as hair that short can get.

Gavin's face falls into tough lines. He rises from behind the desk. "Can I help you, pal?"

Detective Riordan doesn't seem to hear him. He stares straight at you. "Oh, *hell* no!" he says. "You are not getting involved with some handsome PI romantic interest. Not on my dime. Get the hell back over to the main storyline."

"Excuse me?"

"Don't give me that wide-eyed, innocent look. You know damn well —" He breaks off.

You say, "I know damn well *what*?"

Astonishingly, he seems choked with emotion. Or maybe it's just choler at the idea that someone would dare argue with him.

"Listen, pal." Gavin starts to come around the desk. "I don't know who you are or what you think you're doing here —"

Riordan gives you a direct and dark look. "On your head," he warns.

"Gavin," you say quickly. "Wait." You stand too. Your heart is pounding fast, your mouth is actually dry. "Okay," you tell Riordan. "What am I missing?"

"Everything," he says. "Some of it, you're just as well off without. But some of it…you don't want to miss. I know you don't, because I don't want to miss it either. As hard and as painful as it's going to be — and believe me, there are moments coming that you'll think are going to break you — I wouldn't trade any of it. Not a minute. Because." He comes to another of those sudden stops.

"Because why?" you whisper.

Why are you whispering? *Because nobody should hear this except the two of you?*

"Because we get something most people don't get."

"That could mean a lot of things," you point out. "It could mean Willie Wonka chocolate bars. It could mean we both develop the same rare disease. In fact, that's kind of how it sounds. You're going to have to say it. The words matter. One word in particular."

"Love," Riordan says. "We get love. And we get it for a long time — longer than either of us thought we'd have. But that's not what I mean. That's not the rare thing."

He looked so angry, so dangerous when he burst into Gavin's office, but somehow you've covered that distance of floor and carpet and you're standing right in front of him, gazing into his eyes, and you're not afraid of him. Maybe a little afraid of some of what lies ahead, but not of him. Not of Jake.

"So what's the rare and special part?"

"We understand what we have. And not a day goes by that we don't remember it." He's watching you, waiting to see if you understand.

Gavin says suddenly, skeptically from behind you, "You're saying you live happily ever after?"

"I'm not saying that," Jake says. "For all I know, you'd actually be happier with him." He nods at Gavin, but his tawny gaze never leaves your own. "It would sure as hell be easier with him."

It's funny that the smile seems to start in your chest and work its way muscle by muscle to your face. You can feel that smile coming long before it curves your mouth, and you say gravely, "But?"

"He won't feel a fraction of what I do for you. You won't change his life. And you will always wonder about what could have been, always feel that funny little ache right here." He puts his hand over your heart.

You feel that touch right through your shirt. Feel the warmth of his tenderness, the weight of his possession.

You put your hand over his, and he captures it. You smile. Does he realize you're holding hands? Maybe he does, because he raises your clasped hands, and gives your knuckles a quick kiss. Not a smooth move, not a practiced move, but if you wanted smooth and practiced, you'd stay in this office with the fake Maltese falcon in the foyer and the Bombay Company knock-off furniture.

You let Jake lead the way out of the office, down the stairs, and back to the busy street below.

The End

You're very fond of your dear old mum, but there's no denying these little get-togethers are hard on your nerves.

Your mother breaks the news to you that yet another of your old high school friends died recently. Rusty Corday fell out of a high rise hotel in Buffalo.

When you return to Cloak and Dagger Books, Angus informs you that you just missed the police. Or, more exactly, Detective Riordan.

Weirdly, you're not sure if that's a relief or a disappointment.

Angus also lets you know that flowers were delivered for you earlier in the afternoon.

The flowers are in one of those long white florist boxes. You've never had flowers sent to you before, and you could have done without these. Black hollyhocks and a dozen blood-red roses, perfect to the last thorn, seem a little on the macabre side.

There's a card though no signature.

Nothing to him falls early, or too late...

You bin the flowers only to find Angus lurking behind you in the kitchen. He tells you Claude has been trying to reach you all day.

You call Claude who immediately launches into a tirade about how you led the police straight to him. Once you calm him down, he begins to talk about Robert, and what he has to say is not reassuring. As much as you hate to believe it, Claude sounds like he had a pretty strong motive for killing Robert.

But Claude also points out that Robert wasn't the most tactful or sensitive of souls, and he made a lot of enemies. That's true. You knew Robert a long time. You practically grew up together. Feeling a little nostalgic, you dig out your own yearbook and flip through the pages of youthful faces.

Angus calls you to the phone, but when you pick up, there's no one there.

Is it just me or is a lot of stuff happening to you all at once?

Anyway, you're having cereal for dinner because you are one Lonely Guy, when Detective Riordan shows up unannounced.

If you decide to let Jake in,
turn to page 96

If you decide it would be wiser not to answer the door
and instead catch up on your paperwork,
turn to page 93

Five minutes later, after proceeding along an inclined gallery that winds ever upward, you're ushered into a vast vaulted chamber lit with a thousand phosphorescent lamps and gleaming with idols of gold and silver, jewels flashing from their eyes.

High in the dome hangs a great golden disc, representing the sun. At the far end, above a marble altar, coils a dragon with tusks of ivory and scales of jade, its eyes two lustrous pearls. And all about the room throng priests in fantastic head-dress and long white robes, woven through elaborately with threads of yellow and green.

At the appearance of the captives — that would be you and Professor James Riordan — a murmur like a chant rises in the still air. Someone touches a brand to the altar and there is a flash of flame followed by a thin column of smoke that spirals slowly upward.

Now one of the priests steps out — the supreme one among them, to judge from the magnificence of his robe — and addresses you, speaking slowly, rhythmically.

As his strange, sonorous discourse continues, Professor Riordan grows visibly perturbed. His blond beard twitches and he shifts uneasily on his feet.

Finally the discourse ceases and the professor replies to it, briefly. He turns his grave, tawny eyes on you.

"What is it?" you ask quietly. "What did the priest say?"

He considers, before replying.

"Naturally, I did not gather everything," is his slow reply, "but I gleaned sufficient information to understand what is afoot. First, however, let me explain that the dragon you see over there embodies their deity Tlaloc, god of the sea. In more happy circumstances, it would be interesting to note that the name is identified with the Mayan god of the same element."

He pauses, as though loath to go on, then continues, "At any rate, the Antillians have worshipped Tlaloc principally, since their sun god failed them. They believe he dragged down their empire in his mighty coils, through anger with them, and will raise it up again if appeased. Therefore they propose today to —"

A chill ripples down your spine. "Uh, that's interesting." You unobtrusively check how many rounds of ammo remain in your belt. "But does that mean what I think it does?"

"Not being a mind reader, I can't be sure, however, if you surmise that we are about to be sacrificed to the dragon god of the Antillians, I concur."

"Oh. Okay. Well, have you any brilliant ideas as to how we can get out of this jam, Professor?"

"Hey, this is all you," Professor Riordan says, turning his bespectacled gaze your way. "You fell asleep doing paperwork and now you're having another one of your kinky dreams. I'm just along for the ride." He coughs politely into his fist. "My suggestion is you wake up and retrace your way back to the main storyline. I can assure you with some degree of confidence that this particular branch is not going to end well..."

You get a couple of beers and Detective Riordan sits down at your kitchen table. He reminds you that you're supposed to be helping save your sorry ass by figuring out the connection between Hersey and that chess piece.

Well, you didn't think this was a social call, right?

You suggest that Robert died at the hands of a serial killer, but Riordan brushes the idea off — even though he's the one who brought the chess piece to your attention. And if a chess piece clutched in a dead man's hand doesn't seem like serial killer territory, you don't know what does. Then again, you read a lot of mysteries. Riordan probably does not. It's doubtful he knows how to read at all.

Which doesn't change the fact that he's a good-looking son of a bitch. And, while he does seem irrefutably straight, you can't quite shake that sense that there's some connection between you.

You do get him to finally admit he doesn't think you killed Robert, and that means a lot since his partner, Chan, does think you did it. And most of the evidence, such as there is, points to you.

You remind Riordan that Robert had met someone new, that there was a new man in his life — a man no one seems to know anything about. "Find the guy Robert went to meet that night and I think you'll nail whoever killed him."

Riordan is not impressed. "Did you know Claude La Pierra, aka Humphrey Washington, has a juvenile arrest sheet as long as your arm?"

You did not know that.

Riordan has a second beer, you chat about murder and mayhem some more and then he gets up to leave.

If you impulsively choose to ask Riordan to stay,
turn to page 100

If you see Riordan to the door
and then you trundle off to bed,
turn to page 98

On Monday Tara shows up at the bookstore to give you Rob's old high school yearbook. She says that Robert requested she send it to him a few weeks before his death. Surely that means *something* because Rob had a couple of old yearbooks at his apartment, which means he must be searching for something in particular? Something pertaining to a specific year?

Right after she leaves, Claude calls with some startling news."I saw him, *cherie*, last night at Ball and Chain."

It takes you a few seconds to get the gist of it, but it turns out Claude has recognized Detective Riordan as a regular at a sex club called Ball and Chain.

"He was probably undercover or something."

"No! You're not listening to me. I've seen him there before. He's a *member*. He's a *master*."

Claude begins to babble about Robert visiting that same club sometimes, which — in Claude's opinion — makes Riordan a suspect in Robert's death. Claude seems to believe he can parlay this information to his own advantage, perhaps get Riordan thrown off the case or, better still, blackmail Riordan into backing off in his investigation. You may not be an expert on human nature, but even you can tell Riordan is not the backing off kind.

You try and explain this to Claude, but he misreads your concern for him as concern for Detective Riordan. Which is just...weird. You don't even like Riordan. At least, you don't think so. He's kind of a hard person to like, seeing that he thinks you're capable of murder.

Claude hangs up on you, and no sooner do you replace the receiver than that reporter from *Boytimes*, Bruce Green, shows up and asks if he can buy you a cup of coffee.

You let Green know that you've done some checking and you've discovered he doesn't actually work for *Boytimes*, but he explains that he's a freelancer.

Which...well, that's possible, after all.

If you choose to go have coffee with Green,
turn to page 114

If you suddenly feel like you need a nap,
turn to page 110

You're out of practice, so it isn't smooth. "Look, you don't have to leave. I mean, unless you do. But if you don't have to be anywhere...I'd like you to stay." You're not even sure if that's true. Except, strangely, it is. You feel some connection to Riordan. It's crazy, but there's something there.

But maybe it's just on one side.

Riordan's face changes, grows ugly, dangerous. "Stay? What, here? With you?"

He sounds appalled, but there's a certain hungry glitter in his eyes. The heat rushes into your face, but you nod.

He says finally, slowly, "What do you think I am?"

"I...think you're a man. Like me."

He shoves you back, hard. You crash into the hall table, knocking it over, smashing the jar of old marbles you've collected through the years. Glass balls skip and bounce along the corridor. You land on your back, your head banging down on the hardwood floor.

From a distance you hear him saying, "I'm nothing like you!"

For a second or so you lie there, blinking up at the lighting fixture, taking in the years of dust and dead moths gathered in the etched-glass globe. The silence that follows is more startling than the collision of you and the table and the floor. You can hear Riordan's harsh breathing and, from far away, a marble rolling away down the hall — dying into silence.

Riordan bends over you, and you knock his hands, rolling away and scrambling to your feet. You stay out of reach, watching him warily, waiting for him to launch himself at you again. Can you make it to the phone before he knocks you down again? You can't take him, that's for sure.

Riordan is still staring at you in that stricken, horrified way. In his eyes, you read fear, and with the fear, the urge to knock you down again, to punch, to kick, to silence, to destroy. His hands are clenched by his side. You feel light-headed with anger and outrage — and yeah, you're scared too. He could probably kill you by accident. Or maybe it won't be by accident. Your heart is tripping in your throat.

You can barely form the words without crying. From rage. "Get out."

He swallows once, dryly. He looks sick. He opens his mouth, closes it.

You harden your voice. "I won't tell you again. Get out."

In the back of his too bright eyes, you see the thoughts flitting through his brain. If he leaves, if you report this assault, he might lose his job. Worse, it might provoke speculation into something he very much does not want anyone to speculate on. Ever. The very thing *you* speculated on.

He could shut you up for good. With one well-placed punch, he could probably solve the problem of you. He could claim you admitted to killing Robert and that you tried to jump him.

There is fear and desperation in his face. Riordan is right to be afraid because you don't know yourself what you plan to do — if you live through the next two minutes.

The seconds pass. Your gaze never wavers from Riordan's.

Then he goes, shutting the door quietly behind him.

If you phone the police and report the assault,
turn to page 112

If you decide to keep your mouth shut about the assault,
turn to page 117

Finally you decide that since you're probably not going to live that long anyway, it'll be less trouble for everyone if you just move in with your mother for however much time you have left.

Lisa hires an overpriced team of specialists to oversee your "recovery," even though the possibility for actual recovery is nil. In addition to a night nurse, a masseur, and a physical therapist, she hires a day nurse by the name of Jean Paul.

Jean Paul is six foot three, French and totally gorgeous. He is a few years younger than you and professes to be a fan of your book, which is probably total bullshit, but one day when you're in one of your rare pleasant moods, the two of you start talking about Georges Simenon and French mystery fiction, and it turns out that Jean Paul really has read your book.

After this you start to see Jean Paul as a person rather than simply a strong back and a muscular pair of arms.

You're not sure what Jean Paul sees when he looks at you — other than a patient with SCI and a weak heart. It's impossible for you to believe that anyone would want you now, so you feel safe opening up to him about things you wouldn't share with anyone else. He's surprisingly easy to talk to. Maybe it's a French thing, but Jean Paul seems absolutely unshockable.

At first Jean Paul is just a sympathetic and sensible listener, but eventually he opens up to you as well, talking about his childhood in Provence, working in the vineyards, his immigration problems, and the challenges of being a gay man in the nursing profession.

"Are you in a relationship?" you ask him one morning when he's taking your blood pressure.

"*Non*," Jean Paul says absently, reminding you of your old friend Claude. "I am, as you would say, married to my work." He teases, "I am married to you, Adrien."

Jean Paul pumps the blood pressure cuff, looks surprised at the reading, and meets your eyes. You feel yourself blushing, though you try to tell yourself you were just making *la* conversation.

Later you lie in the bathtub, while Jean Paul bathes your motionless body. Not entirely motionless as your chest does continue to rise and fall, whether you like it or not. It is so strange to see him lift your foot and scrub the sole with the little clear nail brush, but feel nothing. The scented water laps against you, the bubbles snap and dissipate against your pale skin, but it could all be happening to someone else. Your body doesn't even look like your body anymore. You close your eyes because you hate the sight of the useless carcass that is you.

When you open your eyes again, Jean Paul is holding your cock in his well-shaped hand and gently washing you. He handles you like you are beautiful and precious, and it is infuriating that you cannot feel his touch. But then a crazy thing happens. Your cock hardens.

You still can't feel it — and your erection doesn't last — but Jean Paul looks at you and smiles widely. "Oh ho *ho*," he says. It is a distinctly French sound.

You laugh. "I wish —"

You don't finish the thought, but Jean Paul studies you with his bright blue eyes. "*Moi aussi*," he says softly.

Your relationship changes subtly but importantly after this, and you begin to spend more and more time with Jean Paul. When he mentions looking for a new apartment, you suggest to Lisa that you would like Jean Paul to be around more, and she invites him to move into the Porter Ranch house as your fulltime "companion."

It's a nice old-fashioned word to cover up the fact that your former friends and acquaintances don't have time for you now. Or maybe Lisa keeps them away. Sometimes you would prefer to believe that.

Anyway, Jean Paul agrees — probably because Lisa bribes him heavily with free room and board on top of his already generous salary.

You tell yourself you're a realist. You know this is a paid gig for Jean Paul, but he's kind and attentive and you have to take what you can get. You're grateful. Mostly. Sometimes you're resentful, and unlike Jean Paul, you're not always kind. But Jean Paul doesn't seem to mind.

You quickly become inseparable. Which only means he knows what side of the bread his butter is on.

One autumn afternoon Jean Paul takes you out into the garden and lifts you out of your chair, lying beside you on the green grass and golden leaves. It's wonderful. The grass tickles your neck and the earth smells warm and alive. Jean Paul kisses you sweetly and then he spends the next half hour making love to you.

Before your accident you would never have believed how much pleasure could come from having your face and hair caressed. Jean Paul gives you butterfly kisses with his eyelashes and nibbles on your ears and sucks on your lower lip. At the same time his hand moves slowly and patiently on your cock. You can't feel it and yet you're enjoying the experience. You enjoy it more when his face tightens and you watch him come with a quiet, ferocious intensity.

"Mon Dieu!" he gasps. It's not at all corny, though it should be. He buries his face against you and says something. The words are muffled, but it almost sounded like he says, *"Je t'aime, je t'aime..."*

"What?"

He raises his head, smiles at you, and goes back to working your cock, which is now startlingly erect. Jean Paul chuckles and kisses the head of your cock as though it is his little *bon ami.* After a time, you experience a prolonged, almost euphoric sense of relaxation... It's hard to describe, but you know exactly what it is.

You've had an orgasm. The first one since your accident two years earlier. You didn't think that was possible, but Jean Paul kisses your trembling mouth and damp eyes and earnestly explains about "transfer orgasm" and "neural plasticity."

You pretend to listen to him, but the only thing that really sticks is the memory of his soft, broken words. *"Je t'aime, je t'aime..."*

The End

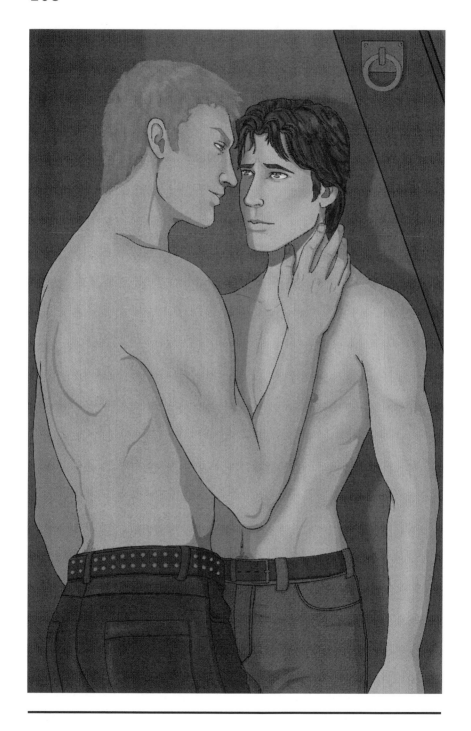

SERIOUSLY? You have a heart condition and you decide to give chase to a masked prowler in a deserted alley only days after one of your friends was carved up like a Thanksgiving turkey?

I don't think so.

Get your ass back over to page 145

If you suddenly feel like you need a nap,
turn to page 110

Then Arlok contemptuously flings you away from him. As you stagger backward, Arlok's tentacle lashes upward and levels upon you. Once more the twin tips glow brilliant green and livid blue. Instantly every muscle in your body is paralyzed. You stand there as rigid as a statue, your body completely deadened from the neck down. Beside you, Jake is also frozen motionless by that same weird power.

"Earthling, you are beginning to try my patience," Arlok snaps. "Can you not realize that I am utterly invincible in any combat with you? The living metal of my body weighs over sixteen hundred pounds, as you measure weight. The strength inherent in that metal is sufficient to tear a hundred of your Earth men to shreds. But I do not even have to touch you to vanquish you. The electric content of my bodily structure is so infinitely superior to yours that with this tentacle-organ of mine I can instantly short-circuit the feeble currents of your nerve impulses and bring either paralysis or death as I choose.

"But enough of this!" Arlok breaks off abruptly. "My materials are now ready, and it is time that I finished my work. I shall put you out of my way for a few hours until I am ready to send you through the Gate to the laboratories of Xoran."

The green-and-blue fire of the tentacle's tips flames to dazzling brightness. The paralysis of your body sweeps swiftly over your brain. Black oblivion engulfs you.

"Adrien! Psst! ADRIEN!"

You open your eyes.

"You're doing it again," Jake whispers. "Not that the blue-and-green tentacle-organ thing doesn't have some real possibilities, but if you really want to try something kinky, I have a suggestion..."

Your hands are shaking as you phone your local police department and report the assault.

You're half prepared for them to blow you off, especially given that you're a suspect in Riordan's murder investigation, but that doesn't happen. That very evening two plainclothes detectives arrive and take your report. You're still angry and humiliated and you give them the complete and unvarnished truth of everything that has occurred between you and Detective Riordan since the moment he walked into your bookstore.

From that point on, things happen very quickly and even if you wanted to stop the unraveling sequence of events, you couldn't.

Riordan is removed from the Gay Slasher case and Chan is partnered with a junior detective by the name of Alonzo. Chan still believes you're their perp, but despite the two of them doing their very best to measure you for a pair of stainless steel bracelets, they can't come up with enough evidence for an arrest.

Through the grapevine you learn that Riordan has been suspended from LAPD, and then a few weeks later, you hear he's been arrested for Robert's murder. Once IA started investigating him, the trail led straight to his extracurricular activities and it turned out he had a couple of encounters with Robert at an unsavory club called Ball and Chain.

Eventually he's convicted of Robert's murder and sent to San Quentin.

You're not sure if he killed Robert or not, but he seemed to have a lot of faith in the system, so hopefully he feels justice was done.

A few nights after you learn of Riordan's sentencing, you're working alone in the back room of the bookstore when a man wearing a skull mask and wielding a butcher's knife bursts in. You're cornered in the stock room. You try tipping a bookshelf on your assailant, but there's no escape. As the knife plunges into your chest the first time, you wonder what former detective Riordan is doing this evening...

The End

You end up going for a drink at a little Scottish-themed pub. It's a quiet little place with red-and-black tartan carpet and blackened beams. You settle in a large leather booth in the back and order a Drambuie.

Bruce — yes, you're on a first-name basis now — surprises you by confessing that he's *not* going to write "your" story for *Boytimes* because LAPD has another prime suspect in mind now. His interest in you is purely personal.

You're flattered. Mostly. You're also startled. It's been a long time since another man has shown a personal interest in you. In fairness, you haven't made it easy for anyone to show an interest in you. In fact, you're probably well on your way to turning into one of those weird, old, eccentric book collectors — and you're only thirty-two. You haven't had a date in eight months.

Bruce is attractive in an awkward but well-groomed way. Okay, he wears Giorgio for Men, but nobody's perfect. At least he's open and honest about his interest. In fact, he admits he's been looking into your background. Which would be a little creepy if he wasn't a reporter and hadn't been planning to do an article on you.

"Am I coming on too strong?" he asks. "I feel like there's kind of a connection between us. I felt it that first day. At the funeral. Is it just me?"

The truth is, you're not sure. You did feel a kind of recognition when you first saw him.

Anyway, you finish your Drambuie and then you go home and you spend a few hours drinking and thinking, which is how you spend a lot of evenings. Only tonight your thoughts are about Robert and who might have killed him.

Tara certainly had motive. Robert abandoned her and his kids in order to run off and "find himself." Plus, she is the beneficiary of his big, fat, life insurance policy.

Claude seems to be nursing both a broken heart and some bitter feelings. Plus he's acting totally guilty.

Then there was that mystery man Robert had been seeing in the weeks before his death.

And there is Detective Riordan. If Claude is right and Riordan did run into Robert at that leather club, well... it's a possibility, right? Not a possibility you want to think about...

And maybe right there, that's worth noting.

If you decide to get dressed and head over to
Ball and Chain to do some amateur sleuthing,
turn to page 133

If you decide to keep on with the thinky-think stuff,
turn to page 143

Nᴏᴛ ᴛʜɪs ᴘᴀɢᴇ!!!!!

You're not sure why you decide to keep your mouth shut. Partly it's embarrassment, of course. Having to explain to Riordan's fellow police officers that you propositioned him? What if they agree with his reaction? What if they don't believe you? And even if they do, you'd maybe have to testify at a hearing or a trial? Oh hell no.

But partly...

You're sorry for Riordan. As crazy as that sounds — and is — you're sorry for him. You feel sick when you remember the terrified confusion in his eyes. He looked like a trapped animal.

So you don't file assault charges. You keep your mouth shut.

You don't see Riordan for several days. You don't hear anything from the cops at all. But then, after you discover that the lunatic who broke into your shop left a dead cat hidden in the stock room, Chan shows up with Riordan in tow.

You explain the situation and Riordan and Chan exchange The Look. Once again it is painfully clear they don't believe you. They think you've concocted this sick scenario to throw suspicion off yourself. They must think you're a complete moron, and that makes you even angrier than them thinking you're a killer.

"If people would be candid to start with, it would help," is all Chan responds to your angry outburst.

"*I'm* not being candid? I am a victim here. I am being stalked."

"Run that by me again," Riordan requests. It's the first time he manages to meet your gaze directly.

"I am being stalked," you tell him.

"Who do you think is stalking you, Mr. English?" Chan asks politely, unwrapping a stick of gum.

You drag them upstairs and show them Rob's yearbook, delivered by Tara. You tell them about Rusty Corday maybe or maybe not committing suicide.

Chan is unimpressed. "In any high school graduation class there's going to be a number of deaths, suicides, even homicides by the time your tenth reunion rolls around. It's the law of averages."

Riordan is noncommittal.

Chan says, "This book of yours that's going to be published; it's about a man who stabs to death an old friend, isn't it?"

"Actually, it's about a man who finds out who stabbed to death an old friend. He's an amateur sleuth."

"He's a homosexual," Riordan says.

"Yeah, well, we all know you've got some issues there, Detective," you say.

There's an uncomfortable silence. Riordan stares at you with dark, fathomless eyes.

Chan changes the subject hastily. He mentions Tara is the beneficiary of Robert's insurance policy. Riordan points out that apparently Robert didn't feel stalked before his murder. So it's full circle. As far as Riordan and Chan are concerned, your stalker and Robert's murder are not connected.

Or, more precisely, you're making up the whole stalker thing.

They leave and you start to get ready to go have dinner with Jean and Ted, but then you hear the downstairs buzzer.

You run downstairs and who should be fidgeting on your doorstep, but Mr. Law and Disorder himself.

"What do you want now?" you demand.

Riordan tugs unconsciously at his collar. He says gruffly, "Can I talk to you?"

"Talk."

He glares, but then his gaze falls. "I owe you an apology. For the other night."

"You do, yeah."

His lashes lift. His eyes look almost green in the evening light. "I'm genuinely sorry for what happened. There's no excuse for it, so I'm not going to waste your time trying to come up with one. I've never done anything like that before."

"Really? Because it seemed — felt — pretty instinctive to me."

"No. I've never used unauthorized force on a civilian. This was assault. I committed assault." He seems genuinely appalled even now, remembering it. "You should have reported me, but I'm grateful that you didn't."

You shrug uncomfortably.

"I want you to know that the morning after it happened, I made an appointment with the department shrink."

"You did?" That does surprise you.

Riordan nods. "What you said was true. I've got some unresolved issues. But I'm working on them. I just wanted you to know that. And to know that I'm sincerely sorry for shoving you."

"Even if I am a murderer?"

He grimaces. "I don't think you're a murderer. You know that wasn't the reason."

"I know."

He gives you another one of those pained, guilty looks. "I could have really hurt you, Adrien. I'm very much aware of that."

You smile, surprising yourself. "It's okay. Only my ego was dented."

His gaze softens and he says seriously, "Your ego should still be intact. If anything, I reacted *because* —" He breaks off but you can still follow his line of thought.

"Oh," you say. And then *"Oh?"*

He smiles faintly. "Yeah. Anyway, I just needed to let you know that nothing like that will ever happen again. You have my word."

"All right. Thank you. I appreciate the apology."

He nods curtly and turns away. You close the door firmly.

You don't see Detective Riordan for a few days and by then things have changed pretty dramatically. You're dating Bruce, Claude has informed you that Riordan is not only gay, he's involved in the BDSM scene, and then Claude himself is murdered.

Riordan shows up right after the crime scene people arrive. "How are you doing?" he asks, and he seems genuinely concerned in his terse way.

You're dismayed by how much you want to believe his concern is genuine. After all, you know first hand what a violent temper he has. Claude tried to blackmail Riordan and now Claude is dead. Coincidence? It seems unlikely.

"Still kicking," you say, or words to that effect.

"You feel up to making a statement?"

Not really. In fact, your chest is tight, your left arm is numb, and your heart is skipping every couple of beats. But you're more afraid of dragging attention to your physical frailties than you are of having a heart attack, so you nod.

Riordan gives you a measuring look. "Let's step over here." He gives you his suede jacket and he has you sit in his car while he questions you.

You try to stay calm, but you've just come face to face with a murderer and lost one of your best friends. And you're not absolutely sure that Riordan isn't somehow part of this. You don't want to think it, but...

You tell him everything that happened. He doesn't take notes. Why? He just listens to you, nodding slowly to himself. It's just you and him. No one else can hear your conversation, and that worries you too. Why has he taken you out of earshot of the other crime scene personnel?

Meanwhile, he keeps picking and pulling at your story. "Skull mask? You mean like the mask you saw on the prowler outside your apartment?"

You assent.

"Or do you think you saw something, say a white ski mask, and your mind made the connection?"

"No."

"You said yourself it all happened pretty fast."

"I know what I saw. A skull mask. Like you buy at Halloween. The same mask. The same man. Hefty. Your height. Your build." You can't control your voice. You start to shake.

Riordan watches you like you're something unpredictable and dangerous. "Okay. Bring it down a notch, Adrien."

"See, I have this problem," you tell him. "There is such an obvious link between everything that has happened that a blind man could see it, but somehow you don't see it. So I am asking myself, why don't you see it? Because you don't want to? Or because you don't want anyone else to?"

"Lower your voice."

You do lower your voice but that's because you can't catch your breath. In fact, you're really in trouble now, and you know it. Your body is bathed in cold sweat. Pain radiates from your shoulder all the way down your left arm. There's a crushing weight on your chest and you feel a sense of impending doom.

"What's wrong?" Detective Riordan asks from a long way away. "Adrien?"

"Heart," you gasp out. "My heart..." You close your eyes. Your voice is thin and faraway and you're afraid he doesn't hear you. Or maybe he hears you but he will choose to do nothing about it...

But no.

Next time you open your eyes you're in a hospital bed. You learn you've had a massive heart attack and you've lost one-third of your heart's function, but you're alive thanks to the quick thinking and quick acting of Detective Riordan. When Riordan realized what was happening to you, he drove you straight to the nearest hospital, sirens screaming, lights flashing.

Er, that would be the car, not Riordan, although according to the nurses, Riordan was pretty damned upset and insistent the doctors save you.

And save you they did. So now you're busy recovering, which is a slow, painful process. There's no use denying that you're frightened. You nearly died and your heart is in bad shape. Thanks to your mother and all her filthy lucre, you're receiving the best possible treatment, but the prognosis after a massive heart attack is not good.

On the other hand, the fact that you survived at all is very good news. So you might as well look on the bright side.

Preoccupied with your own problems, you don't give a lot of thought to poor Claude's murder — or even Robert's. But then one afternoon Detective Riordan shows up. You think at first he's there to question you yet again, but no. He's brought you a couple of Mark Cohn CDs and a book on police procedure.

"You don't look as bad as I expected," says Riordan, ever the silver-tongued devil. He takes one of those uncomfortable plastic chairs and drags it next to your bed. You've just returned from your morning stroll, such as it is, and you're feeling tuckered out and peevish. Still...you're kind of glad to see him. More glad than you expected.

"You're too kind." You study the book. *Basic Criminal Law: The Constitution, Procedure, and Crimes.* "What's this for?"

"I read your manuscript. I thought you could use a good resource or two."

You laugh for the first time in nearly two weeks. He smiles too. A crooked sort of grin.

You say, "I guess I should thank you for saving my life."

"Not if it hurts that much."

You pull a face. "Yeah, well, I am grateful. Mostly. Thank you."

He shrugs. "We're even. You spared my life, I saved yours."

"I don't think I actually spared your life," you feel obliged to point out.

"I think you probably did," Riordan says. "Anyway, I've been going through your notes on the case —"

"You did *what?*"

He looks uneasy. "Hey. You're not supposed to get excited."

"You went through my papers?"

"I did, yeah. And it turns out you're not just a pretty face."

"No, I've got a useless body too."

He scowls. "Knock it off. I've talked to your doctors. Other than your heart, you're pretty healthy."

"Oh! Well, since it's just my heart!"

"I said knock it off. You're going to recover from this. And it's not like your dreams were pinned on becoming a pro athlete. Anyway, since you're laid up, I thought maybe you could help me out with the case."

"Help you out?" You repeat doubtfully. You're still processing the fact that Riordan talked to your doctors and you're apparently not shuffling off the mortal coil in the immediate future. Everyone has ducked that particular point with you, but maybe Riordan's job has better prepared him for delivering bad news. Or maybe he really does take the optimistic view. You decide to go with his version of events. What the hell do you have to lose?

"Nothing strenuous," he says. "But you know a lot of the principals in this case, so I thought maybe I could come by each day and maybe talk the case over with you."

"Use me as a sounding board?"

"Something like that."

You think it over. You like the idea. A lot, actually. You like the idea of seeing more of Detective Riordan, you like having something to think about besides your own ill health. And, if someone was trying to kill you, you're in a more vulnerable position than ever, so it's to your benefit to get this case solved.

"Okay," you say. "I'll help if I can."

True to his word, Detective Riordan — you come to know him as Jake — shows up every evening to discuss the ongoing case with you. Even after you're released from the hospital and staying at your mother's, he turns up every evening with his case notes.

You usually talk for a few hours, longer than your mother, who plainly fears you're going to keel over any moment, would like. At first you just talk about the case — argue about the case, mostly — but then you start talking about other things including Riordan's therapy and your own experiences as a gay man.

You don't really have a lot in common, although you do laugh a lot and you never seem to run out of things to talk about. You like him. Very much. And he seems to like you. In fact, he starts stopping by on weekends and sometimes you don't talk about his case at all.

Sometimes you go out for a drive together or a walk in the park.

You continue to recover but the doctors tell you you're not ever going to be well enough to go back to running the bookstore. No stress, no strain. Your life has to be very different from here on out, and that's that.

You tell Riordan this, and as you might expect, he's more bracing rather than sympathetic. "So you'll focus on your writing career instead, right?"

"I can't earn a living writing!"

You expect him to say what Lisa always says: you don't need to earn a living. But he says, "How do you know? You've never tried till now."

So you begin work on your second book.

And then Riordan solves Robert's murder. It turns out that Bruce Green, the reporter from *Boytimes*, knew Robert in high school and held some kind of a grudge. He also killed Claude because...well, it's not exactly clear why. Maybe because he was afraid Claude recognized him?

You don't know, because Riordan stops coming to see you.

Just like that.

Case closed and your usefulness is at an end.

It hurts. But you sort of suspected that was going to happen eventually. Despite all the therapy, Jake Riordan hasn't worked out that he's gay yet, and by the time he does work it out, you might not still be around. Or he might not be interested. In fact, he almost certainly won't be interested in you that way. He's going to be looking for someone like himself. Some big, robust asshole he can box with and jog with and knock around when they don't see eye to eye.

You keep working on your second book and the days go by. And then the weeks and then the months.

Your first book is a moderate success and you sell the second book. You begin work on a third book.

And then Mel comes to visit. He's visiting his parents and learned about your heart attack. Of course this is the very reason he bailed on you; he always knew this day was coming. But he's very sweet and very attentive and your ego could use a little nurturing. Mel visits a couple of times.

On Mel's second visit, Jake Riordan shows up unannounced.

Gloria, your mother's housekeeper, shows him out to the pool area where you and Mel are sunning yourselves in the autumn sunshine.

"Sorry, I didn't realize you had company," Riordan says. He looks out of place in his suit and tie. Tall, thinner, a little fine drawn. You feel a twinge of anxiety. Is he okay? He looks tired, grim. Are things not going well for him?

You rise from the lounge chair, going to meet him. "It's just Mel." You almost hug him, but remember in time that he won't want that, so you offer your hand.

He shakes hands briefly. "You look good," he says, light eyes studying your face.

You do look a lot better, thank God. You're almost at your normal weight and you're tanned, which always helps.

"How are you?" you ask. "Would you like a drink?"

Jake declines a drink. He sits down and visits briefly. He talks about the case against Green. He's sure Green will be convicted.

"That's great," you say. It all seems like a really long time ago. "How's the job?"

Jake tells you he's in line for promotion.

"That's great," you parrot again. You wish Mel would go away. This is so uncomfortable and stiff. You can tell

Mel thinks Jake is a typical asshole cop and Jake thinks… it's hard to know what Jake thinks, other than he made a mistake in coming to see you.

After fifteen excruciating minutes Jake excuses himself and departs.

"He sure thinks a lot of himself," Mel remarks as the pool yard gate clangs shut behind Jake. "Why would he think you'd be sitting around waiting for him?"

You look blankly at Mel and then you go after Jake.

He's almost to his car, but he stops when you call to him. He walks back to meet you.

"What's the matter?" he asks, frowning. He reaches out automatically and you grab for him. Not because you need his support but because you welcome the excuse to be in his arms.

"That's what I wanted to ask you. What's wrong?"

"With me? Nothing."

"Bullshit. I know you Jake."

He gives you a strange smile. "You *know* me?" His arms are strong and the support is there if you need it. You don't, but it dawns on you that maybe he likes to be needed. Maybe that's part of why he became a cop.

"I know you that well," you say. "Tell me what's going on, Jake. I want to help."

He stares at you like you're speaking in a foreign language, and then emotion twists his face. "Are you back together with him? After he let you down the last time?"

The naked honesty of that completely disarms you. "No." You shake your head. "No way. We're just friends."

He looks like he's not sure he believes you.

"Why did you stop coming to see me?" you ask.

"I..." There is so much pain in his eyes. It brings tears to your own. No one should hurt that much. It makes your heart ache — in a non-life-threatening way. Jake seems to struggle with himself before he says flatly, "I ran out of excuses."

"Excuses for what? For coming to see me?"

"Yeah." His smile is almost bitter. "Pathetic, isn't it?"

"I don't know. I just know I miss you. So much. I thought we —" But maybe that's more than he's ready to hear. Probably. "We're friends," you say instead.

"Like you and Mel?"

Your heart starts to pound. Probably too hard, but you're going to have this if it kills you. "You know it's not the same."

"I do, yeah."

You stare at each other for a long, long moment.

Jake draws a sharp breath. "I'm sorry. Sorry it took me so long. Sorry I held onto the excuses and the lies. And sorry that after I let go of the excuses and the lies, I still didn't have the guts to face you."

"Until now," you say gently. Because now counts. Every second of it has to count.

"Until now," he agrees. He's gazing down at you almost fiercely, his eyes dark with emotion and longing. You smile at him, and you keep smiling until you see the smile registers. Some of the tension leaves his face.

"Better late than never," you say.

The End

From the outside, Ball and Chain doesn't look so much like a Den of Iniquity as a bar where the booze is liable to be watered down. Of course, it could be both. It's hard to believe anyone who isn't a college student or a senior citizen would have the time and energy for leather-bound high jinks on a week night, but when you finally get the nerve up to go inside, you see that there is a decent crowd.

Er...decent-*sized* crowd.

Er...more people than you expected. You really have no idea what size anyone may or may not be. And probably better not to think about it, since your purpose is strictly of the sleuthiness variety.

It does seem to you that this place would be ideal for a *What Not to Wear* week-long special, but maybe you're feeling bitchy because you're getting some funny looks. Maybe it's the turtleneck. Maybe it's the expression of wide-eyed consternation whenever someone gropes you. You're either being randomly and regularly groped or this is a convention for sufferers of Saint Vitus Dance.

Now that you're here, you're not exactly sure how to proceed. The place is like a warehouse. Both in appearance and purpose. Brick walls, utility lamps, and hot and cold running guys. There is music and it is loud. People are dancing. Hopefully. Did you really think it would be possible to hold a conversation here? Let alone discreetly question someone?

Why are you really here? Wasn't it really curiosity to see what Rob had been up to?

If you're honest...yes. You are curious. You were. Now you're just feeling a little embarrassed and hoping desperately not to meet anyone you kn —

Oh hell no.

Who should you spot from clear across the industrial-sized room but Detective Riordan.

No.

Yes.

Yes. It's really him.

He's standing at the bar drinking whisky and staring broodingly into space. You can't tear your gaze away and you walk right into a cement post.

Fortunately it's only a glancing blow.

You're scrambling to recover your somewhat shaken savoir-faire and look like you really meant to ask that post to dance, when a hand hooks around your arm. You look up and your heart jumps in your chest. Detective Riordan gazes down at you with a strange half smile.

"Well, well, well," he says in that voice that always feels like he's lightly running the tip of a riding crop right down your spine. "Adrien-with-an-e."

"Oh. *Hi*," you say weakly. It really IS him. Detective Riordan is in a leather club. So it's true. Detective Riordan is undercover.

Because he couldn't be gay, right?

Right?

Your gaze falls and you take him in, from the gleam of his black boots...leather jeans...studded leather belt... and then bare, broad muscular chest. Nothing else. Not a single extra anything. Severe and elegant. Beneath the gold dusting of chest hair, his pecs look like rocks. So do his biceps. He's got an abdomen like a washboard. You can't stop staring. Your mouth is dry, your heart bouncing around like those cartoons of Mexican jumping beans.

"Fancy meeting you here," you say.

"And to think I almost didn't bother tonight." His eyes glitter. He's amused. Amused and...

He wants you.

Holy moly. Detective Riordan wants you.

You say cautiously, "Do you come here often?"

He says gravely, "Often enough to make it worth my time."

You hear the echo of your words and blush. He grins, a crooked and deliberately charming grin. He's watching you with unnerving intensity. "Very pretty," he remarks. "Far too pretty to be left running loose." He taps a knowing forefinger under your chin. "Come on."

"Uh..."

Somehow Detective Riordan's hand is clamped possessively on your left butt cheek and you are being steered gently but firmly through the crowd toward the entrance marked PRIVATE.

"Actually, I was just about to leave," you tell him. "I've got a busy day tomorrow. I was just going to have a quick drink and then home to bed."

"Uh huh."

"No, really. This isn't my kind of thing."

He dips his head. His breath is hot against your ear. As noisy as the room is, you hear every syllable. "How do you know?"

"I'm not into organized religion."

He laughs, gives your butt a little squeeze, and you jump.

You really need to make it clear that this is not what you want. But you always were too damned curious for your own good.

Next thing you know you're being scooted into a small, private room. There is no bed, which is disconcerting. There are padded benches and an odd frame thing that reminds you of the dungeon in *Princess Bride*. There is an open cabinet with a staggering assortment of sexual toys and devices.

Is this a communal room or is it Riordan's private office? Which answer would be more reassuring? You can't tear your gaze from the shelves of the cabinet.

"Wow. Bedknobs and broomsticks," you murmur. How the hell do some of those things fit inside the human body? You probably don't want to know. Not firsthand anyway.

Behind you, Riordan makes a sound like he just inhaled one of the benches. When you glance back at him he looks impassive, so maybe you imagined it.

"So what happens now?" You take the initiative in the hope of restoring some sense of balance to the weird dynamic that seems to be developing here.

"Sir," Riordan says lazily.

"Sir?"

"You address me as 'Sir' or 'Master.'"

"Okay," you say politely.

"Sir."

"Got it."

He prompts patiently, "Sir."

You could go on like this all night, but clearly this is a game he has endless patience for. "Yes, sir, sir." you say.

His mouth twitches, but there is an uncomfortable knowingness in his eyes. And in fact, calling Riordan 'Sir,' does sort of give you a funny feeling in your solar plexus. You probably should have eaten dinner.

"Good." He's right behind you, breathing down your neck, crowding into your space. It's uncomfortable and unsettling and, yes, electrifying. "Do you have a safe word?"

"No."

"Sir," he says very gently, and the hair on the nape of your neck rises.

You swallow. "No, sir."

"Pick a safe word."

"No. I mean, 'no' would be my safe word. Sir."

"Pick a different safe word."

"Stop?" you offer.

"Sir." He swats your butt and this time it stings. "Choose again. Now."

"Cobalt, sir."

"Good boy. You may take your clothes off now."

"You know, to be perfectly honest —"

He swats you again. This time you spin around with more than a little irritation. "Okay. Enough. Cobalt."

It's almost worth it to see the look on his face. "Cobalt?"

"You heard me."

"That's your safe word. You only use it when you're —"

"I know. I read. Enough. I'm safe wording."

He seems more perplexed than irritated. "If you don't want this, then why are you here? And don't give me some bullshit about academic curiosity. What are you really here for?"

Fair question. You open your mouth, but you can't exactly tell him you were playing private dick — although by now he probably has the message as to just how private your dick is. And anyway, that isn't exactly the truth. Nor is this totally about Robert. Not really. The truth is, until you heard Riordan was a possible member of this club, it never occurred to you — would never in a million years have occurred to you — to show up here.

You're here for Riordan.

He sees it in your face, as your gaze meets his tawny one, and he looks about as staggered as a man like Riordan can look and still be on his feet.

"You're kidding." He even sounds a little faint.

"No."

His voice goes even deeper, more growly. "It doesn't work like that."

"What are you talking about? We can't just have sex?"

"No, we can't just have sex."

"Why?"

"What do you mean, why? That's not what we do here."

It's your turn to be perplexed. "Sexual intercourse does not take place here?"

Riordan looks exasperated — also a little perturbed. "Of course sexual intercourse takes place. But not...you can have that anywhere."

You flutter your eyelashes and say as winningly as you know how, "I was thinking I kinda want to have it here. With you."

"It doesn't work like that, baby." He's trying to be patient now. Even kind — despite the fact that he's taken a couple of steps back from you like he thinks you're wired with explosives.

"Don't you want to have sex with me?"

He stares at you for so long, and so strangely, that your heart sinks. You really did misread this.

But then he says quietly, "Yes. I would."

"Well then —"

"This isn't the right place or the right time."

"Seriously?" You look around the room. Okay, there's no bed — or even a rug — but it's not like all the necessary equipment isn't present.

Hmm. That long mirror that looks suspiciously two-way is a little concerning.

Riordan shakes his head. "No. Not here." He seems quite serious, and he keeps staring at you as though you only met five minutes ago. "Look, I'll call you," he says, and he puts his arm around your shoulders as though he's going to see you to the door.

Hell. He is going to see you to the door. He's throwing you out.

How can this be? You're not so out of practice you don't recognize desire when you see it.

You can't hide your disappointment. "Spare me," you say. "A simple no thanks will do it."

"No." He stops, gazing into your eyes. "I am going to call you." He bends his head and touches his mouth tentatively to yours. It's such a light brush of mouths, careful and sweet. As though he's never kissed anyone before.

As though he's never kissed a man before.

You stare at him, and he offers you a fleeting smile — you must look fairly astonished — and then he opens the door and leads you down a couple of hallways and then out a fire exit.

This time the kiss he gives you is much more assured, practiced, and then the door closes firmly behind you.

Feeling bemused, you walk across the crowded parking lot to your car. Will Riordan call you? He seemed strangely sincere. Besides, what would he have to gain by lying?

But he's probably not calling you tonight. Tonight you're on your own. As usual.

You unlock the driver's door, and start to slide under the wheel. You automatically glance at the backseat, as would anyone who grew up on a steady diet of mystery novels and cop shows, and to your amazement this time there really is someone lying on your backseat. Even as you realize this, the figure — you have only an impression of a dark raincoat and a scary white mask — surges up, butcher's knife in hand.

You're out of the car and running for the club entrance before he can get out of the backseat. He runs after you, but you yank open the door to the club. There's a blast of music and a wave of sweat and cologne, and then you're inside and pushing through the crowd.

You spot Riordan by the bar.

You reach him, and even before you finish explaining, he's leading the way out the club. He spots your would-be assailant running down the street and he gives chase. Riordan knocks him down, kicks the knife away, and proceeds to beat the hell out of him. When the mask is finally pulled from the beaten man, you're horrified to see it's Bruce Green.

Bruce is arrested, and under interrogation confesses to killing Robert.

Because of the circumstances of his breaking the case, Riordan ends up leaving the police force. He opens a private detective office. He does keep his word and he calls you. You end up going out for dinner, one thing leads to another, and before long you're dating steadily. He teaches you a couple of neat tricks that can be done with handcuffs.

The End

Anyway, next thing you know, it's Tuesday and an In Sympathy card arrives in the mail for you. The inscription is the usual stuff, but someone has written beneath in black calligraphy:

> *Our acts our angels are —*
> *For good or ill*

Not Shakespeare; you know your Shakespeare pretty well, thanks to those Jason Leland mysteries you write in your spare time. Bacon? Marlowe?

You leave a message for Detectives Riordan and Chan, but you don't hear anything from them. You don't hear anything from Claude either.

Partners in Crime meets on Tuesday and Claude doesn't show up.

The meeting goes fine. Afterwards, Bruce calls, but you don't pick up. You're not sure why exactly. Maybe you've just gotten used to being lonely.

You flip through Robert's yearbook — he must have asked Tara to send it to him for some reason, right? — and as you examine the photos from the Chess Club, you realize that both Robert and Rusty were members. Not just Robert and Rusty...

Robert Hersey, Andrew Chin, Grant Landis, Richard Corday, Felice Burns, and Not Pictured — Adrien English.

You sit there, Mr. Not Pictured, staring at the black-and-white photo.

144

How the hell could Robert's death have anything to do with what had happened back in high school?

Then again, both Robert and Rusty are dead. Murder and suicide. Two violent deaths. Surely that couldn't be a coincidence, not with Robert found holding a chess piece?

Your speculations are disrupted by commotion in the alley outside. You go to the window and push back the lace drapery. You stare down at the moonlit alley. Light lances off the lids of the trash dumpsters against the back wall. Everything else lies in shadow.

It's very quiet. This part of town is all but deserted at this time of night.

A shadow detaches itself from the darkness. A figure steps into view and gazes up at you. He wears a mask. A grinning skull. He gives you a jaunty little salute and springs away out of sight.

Amateur sleuthing notwithstanding, your heart isn't strong, and this kind of shock is exactly what your doctors have warned you about.

If you decide to pursue this masked prowler,
turn to page 109

If you decide to phone the police and
let them do what they're paid to do,
turn to page 145

The police arrive — just uniformed officers, not your boyfriend Riordan. OH YEAH, YOU KNOW WHAT I'M TALKING ABOUT! DON'T PLAY INNOCENT!

The police are inclined to brush the incident off as kids or pranksters or both.

You try to call Claude, but there's still no reply.

The next morning, the really, really bad smell in the shop, that you haven't previously mentioned in case it's something to do with Angus' digestive issues, reaches crisis point. You search through the shop until you find a trail of ants in the storeroom, leading to an old trunk. You open the trunk and find a dead cat and many, many ants.

You call the police. Uniforms arrive and on their heels, Riordan and Chan.

"What's up?" Riordan asks.

"Someone put a dead cat in the trunk in my office."

Riordan and Chan exchange The Look.

"Who?" Chan asks.

This is where you kind of lose it. "Who? Is that a routine question? How do I know who? The same person who sent me black flowers and a sympathy card, and broke into my shop, and was skulking around the alley last night!"

"Am I missing something here?" Riordan asks his partner. Chan reaches for a cigarette then recalls himself. He starts patting his pockets for gum.

"If people would be candid to start with, it would help," Chan says.

You give an incredulous laugh. "*I'm* not being candid? I am a victim here. I am being stalked."

"Run that by me again," Riordan requests.

Until you put it into words the notion was nebulous, half-formed, but now you find that you believe it to be the truth. "I am being stalked."

Yeah, well, that doesn't go so well. You show them Rob's yearbook. You tell them what Tara said about Robert asking her to mail it to him right before his death. You turn to the page with the Chess Club and point out Rusty. You explain about his taking a walk out of a hotel window.

"I think his death might be related. Maybe he didn't kill himself."

You do everything but draw them a diagram. They remain unconvinced. Or at least, Riordan is unconvinced. Chan is downright disbelieving.

The light goes on. (It's just a metaphor, you're still mostly in the dark — and so are the cops.) "Oh, I get it," you say. "You still think I could be doing this to myself. That I'm trying to throw you off my trail. Red herrings, right?"

Chan says, "That's a good point, Mr. English. This book of yours that's going to be published, it's about a man who stabs to death an old friend, isn't it?"

In short, things go from bad to worse. Not so worse that they arrest you, but it continues to feel like that might just be a matter of time.

You go to Jean and Ted Finch for dinner and they bring up the thing with Max. Yeah, I don't remember who Max is either. It actually doesn't matter.

On the drive home you happen to spot Detective Riordan standing in line for a movie with a red-haired girl. That redhead will be trouble, mark my words.

When you get home, Bruce has left another message. This time you call him back and chat for a few minutes in your underwear, which may or may not be significant. You make plans for the following night.

The next day, you start trying to locate other members of your high school Chess Club. It's a slow process and you don't have any luck.

Your mother calls and you find out that Chan and Riordan are still actively investigating you. They're currently checking into your finances which are a little overstretched, but not to the point where you're actually considering knocking off your old playmates.

You decide you need to up your own efforts to save yourself, and you go visit Max at his little house on Ventura Blvd. Basically, you learn more stuff about Robert you'd have been happier not knowing.

When you get back to Cloak and Dagger Books, Claude calls and says he was held for questioning for a couple of

148

days by the police. But the police had to let him go due to insufficient evidence, and he's planning to leave town. He needs cash fast.

If you decide to meet Claude,
turn to page 153

If you're feeling lucky, turn to page 11

When you finally get back to Cloak and Dagger Books, you discover that you've been robbed. Not only did the thieves swipe the piddling amount of cash in the register, they ransacked the shop. You call the police, but who should show up but Detectives Chan and Riordan.

Every time you look at Riordan, you remember that crazy kiss in Robert's apartment. He, on the other hand, seems as impassive as ever. Although his gaze does have a tendency to shy from yours. Probably because it's obvious Detective Chan believes you faked this burglary and Riordan could — should — alibi you, but isn't doing so.

You open your mouth to point out why you couldn't have faked this break-in, but it probably isn't a great idea to admit to breaking into Robert's apartment. You decide to keep your mouth shut for now and see how it all plays out. Maybe Riordan knows what he's doing.

"They didn't break in." Riordan rejoins Chan at the foot of the stairs and they hold a brief undervoiced conference.

"They must have used Robert's key," you tell them.

Riordan glances up at you. "Yeah, probably."

"Well, I sure as hell didn't fake this break-in." The irritating thing is, that even in this moment of stress, you just can't help noticing how unfairly attractive the asshole is. Long legs encased in Levi's, powerful shoulders straining the seams of a surprisingly well-cut tweed jacket. You wish you could forget how his mouth felt pressing yours.

"Nobody said you did," he says. He asks for your keys in order to check out the upstairs and you can't think of a good reason to refuse. When he returns to the ground floor he shakes his head in answer to Chan's inquiry.

What was he looking for?

"Mr. English," Chan says. "You didn't tell us everything this morning, did you?"

You knew this was coming sooner or later. You say feebly, "I'm not sure what you mean."

Riordan scowls at you like somehow you've let him down.

Chan says, "I was just over at the Blue Parrot. Maybe we should clear up a couple of points."

"Such as why you lied," Riordan chimes in.

It goes downhill from there.

You admit to arguing with Robert over his repeated swiping of the petty cash, but you remind them that that would be a pretty lame motive for murder. Except, as Riordan points out, lots of people kill for lame reasons. MOST people kill for lame reasons.

They try to get you to admit you were sleeping with Robert, but you weren't.

Finally, you say, "Robert left before I did last night. He left to meet someone. Didn't the bartender confirm that?"

Chan snaps his gum. "Sure did. Robert left at 6:45 and you stayed and had a second Midori margarita. You left at about 7:30. Fifteen minutes later, Robert showed up again looking for you."

To your relief, the police do not arrest you. As the door swings shut behind Detective Riordan, you remember you never called

Claude about your aborted attempt to retrieve his letters.

You phone Claude and fill him in on your disastrous attempt at B&B — er, B&E, although every time you think of Riordan...

ANYWAY.

You explain to Claude that the police already found his letters and that it's only a matter of time before they connect "Black Beauty" to him.

Claude is inclined to blame you for this, which is pretty unreasonable. You're about to hang up, but Claude suggests that the two of you try your hand at sleuthing and check out some kinky club Robert used to go to sometimes.

"Uh, I don't think so," you answer. And then, doubtfully, "What kinky club?"

It takes you a few seconds to get the gist of it, but it turns out Claude is talking about some place he refers to as a "leather club" called Ball and Chain.

"You've got to be kidding."

But no, Claude is perfectly serious.

"But I don't have anything to wear," you protest. "Just a dress belt and a few finishing nails and thumb tacks. That's not e —"

"*Ta gueule!*" Claude says, and God knows what that means. Claude probably doesn't. He keeps on and on trying to convince you what a great opportunity this would be to find out who Robert was seeing in the weeks before he was killed.

If you decide to go with Claude to Ball and Chain,
turn to page 161

If you decide to stay home and clean up
your ransacked shop,
turn to page 226

As Fate would have it, Claude insists you meet at the same time you were supposed to be meeting Bruce for your date. You call Bruce to let him know you have to postpone.

"Why are you canceling?"

"I can't — this sounds ridiculous, I know. I can't explain why. Yet."

Another silence. A very bad connection. In more ways than one.

"Yeah. Okay. Well, another time." Bruce sounds extremely cool.

"Bruce, it's something I can't get out of."

"Sure. No problem."

It obviously is a problem. You say, "I'm free Friday. Tomorrow night."

"I'm not."

Ouch. There's actually a lot to be said for being single, and this is one of those things.

You get to the restaurant, which should be packed, but a placard in the window reads CLOSED. The back door is unlocked and you go inside.

You find Claude sitting and smoking in the dark.

"Did you bring the money?"

"No."

"Jesus fucking Christ! Why not?"

154

You try to explain why not. You don't have the money, that's part of it, of course. The other part is you want to stop Claude from making the mistake of his life. But Claude is not in the mood to listen. After nearly braining you with an ashtray, he orders you to leave.

If you choose to get Claude the money,
turn to page 155

If you choose to jump ahead and
see how all this turns out,
turn to page 233

You slip through the back entrance of Café Noir and feel around for the light switch. Fluorescent lights cast hard white light on steel sinks, polished floors, spotless trash pails. Rows of kettles and pots gleam dully above the counters. The smell of disinfectant hangs heavily in the air mixed with the ghostly memory of garlic, basil, thyme, cigarette smoke...and something else.

Something that terrifies you.

You walk toward the dining room entrance. Suddenly, someone hurtles through, crashing into you, knocking you to the glossy floor. You have a glimpse of a black raincoat, a hat pulled low, a skeleton face, a butcher's knife. A scene straight out of a horror movie.

But this freak isn't interested in you. He runs for the back door, raincoat flapping like a scarecrow's overcoat.

"Claude?" you yell. You have a terrible, terrible feeling about this.

You find Claude lying by the front door, a dull puddle widening beneath him, slowly covering the black-and-white checked floor. You kneel beside him, but it's too late to do anything but stay with him as he dies.

The police come at last. Detective Riordan shows up. You remember that Claude said Riordan threatened to kill him. You didn't believe him, but now Claude is dead.

"How are you doing?" Riordan asks. He's watching closely as you nod tightly.

"How's the heart?"

"Takes a licking, keeps on ticking."

The faintest smile touches his mouth. After a moment, he asks, "You want my jacket?"

"Thanks. I'm fine."

He's not impressed. He shrugs out of his suede jacket, tosses it to you, and you fumble it on. It's warm from his body and carries the scent of his soap.

Riordan interviews you briefly and then sends you home.

Bruce phones to apologize and somehow you end up inviting him over. I think we can all do without reliving THAT.

You're letting Bruce out the front entrance when Riordan shows up early the next morning.

You give Bruce a chaste peck under Riordan's inimical eye and then Bruce reluctantly departs so you and Riordan can have coffee and a little chat.

Riordan is dressed casually in jeans, a gray sweatshirt and Reeboks, as though he's on his way to the gym. Which is kind of odd since it gives the appearance he's been lurking outside the bookstore since sunrise.

That could be sinister, right?

I mean, he probably wasn't planning to serenade you.

"For the record," Riordan begins, getting right down to business, "There was no chess piece at the scene. We vacuumed it. Twice."

"Maybe I interrupted him before he could plant it."

"Maybe. But you didn't go to high school with La Pierra did you? La Pierra was never a member of any Chess Club?"

"No."

Riordan seems to believe that Claude's murder is not connected to Robert's, but isn't that a stretch?

You say, "Maybe Claude was killed for another reason."

"Like?"

"He thought he knew who killed Robert."

"And that would be —?"

"You."

But Riordan seems to find this kind of amusing. "You do have balls, English." He drinks his coffee and studies the grapevine stencil on the kitchen walls.

You bring up Claude's theory that Riordan was — is — gay, which provokes a rather unpleasant speech that increasingly upsets readers with each passing year. But hey. Jake is not a politically sensitive guy. Especially back then. Now. Whatever.

"So, do you have relationships with men?" you ask, when you can get a word in.

Riordan answers, "Yeah. I have relationships with men. My father, my brothers, my partner. I have sex with queers. Don't confuse the two."

"Queers and men?"

"Sex and relationships."

"You've never had a healthy, satisfying homosexual relationship." It isn't a question, but he answers anyway.

"That's a contradiction in terms."

So now everybody's on the same page — or at least agreed they are not on the same page and, in fact, aren't even reading from the same book — and you and Riordan get back to discussing the evidence against you. The case against you isn't getting stronger, but it hasn't fallen apart either.

You still believe Robert's killer and your stalker have to be one and the same.Riordan doesn't buy that theory, but he tells you he has done some checking after the remaining members of the Chess Club.

You're not sure if he's telling the truth or just telling you what you want to hear.

Later that afternoon, another creepy present from an anonymous sender arrives for you. A CD of Verdi's *Requiem*.

Apparently, it really is better to give than receive. You hurl the plastic case across the room and it breaks open. Two parts land on the floor. You pick up the CD. Across the front in black Sharpie are printed the words, *"Our fatal shadows that walk by us still."*

It's a quote from "Honest Man's Fortune" by English dramatist John Fletcher.

Man is his own star; and the soul that can
Render an honest and perfect man,
Commands all light, all influence, all fate,
Nothing to him falls early or too late.
Our acts, our angels are, for good or ill
Our fatal shadows that walk by us still.

Which is interesting, but not all that helpful really.

You keep running through the possibilities. Was Robert the victim of a hate crime? Uh...well, yeah. But the other kind of hate crime. Hate Crime.

Could one of Robert's many discarded lovers have taken revenge? But that doesn't explain Claude's death. In fact, as awful as you feel about it now, you kind of suspected Claude of killing Robert.

But now...now you're almost certain that whatever is going on here has ties back to the past, the ancient past. The past you shared with Robert. If you're right, that means Claude was simply...collateral damage. Can that be?

A motive for murder stretching back to adolescence seems far-fetched, but is it more far-fetched than the idea that you're being stalked? Coz you are being stalked.

Whatever the police think or don't think, you know that for a fact.

You continue with your own lame-ass efforts to find the remaining members of your high school Chess Club, and you continue to get nowhere.

You go downstairs and start putting together the next weekend's book signing for Christopher Holmes, the author of the Miss Butterworth and Mr. Pinkerton series. Holmes is gay — and not exactly a people person — so you know you have to prep harder than usual. Luckily his cozy mysteries sell like hotcakes, so the eight people who show up for the signing should be thrilled.

Later that evening, Bruce calls. You're paying bills and being stalked by a psychopath, so you're not in the best mood. Plus...

Well. He's a nice guy and it's lovely to have someone interested and paying attention. Or it *should* be lovely.

But right now you're preoccupied and Bruce's timing could be better. He asks you to dinner.

If you choose to go to dinner with Bruce,
turn to page 168

If you choose to get takeout and
spend an evening at home
turn to page 178

When you climb into Claude's car that evening he says, "*Meechelle, ma belle*, if you were any more vanilla, you would come with a carton of milk."

"Very funny," you say.

"I'm not kidding!"

You lift your leg so he can examine your very expensive leather boots. "My belt is leather," you say.

"*Mon Dieu*," Claude murmurs, and away you go.

If Claude was not with you, you would probably never have the nerve to knock on that heavy wooden door that more than anything resembles the entrance to a dungeon. You realize, of course, that your ideas of what to expect are largely based on Larry Townsend novels and the film *Cruising*. But once you get inside the warehouse — and that is pretty much the ambience, what with the brick walls and utility lamps and guys in jeans and flannel shirts and work boots — it's not that different from any other gay bar you've been in. At least, not on the furthest edges. Which is where you would prefer to stay. But Claude drags you through the heaving surging mass of men wearing way too much cologne. And alcohol.

The music is deafening and about two decades out of date. For some reason, that strikes you as the most embarrassing thing so far. Of course, the night is young. A lot of guys are dancing, and you are reminded yet again that it is sadly true that most white guys, even gay white guys, can't dance.

You avert your gaze from the dreadful spectacle — and who should you spot from clear across the cavern-sized room but Detective Riordan. He's standing at the bar drinking whisky and staring broodingly into space. Your jaw drops and you walk right into a guy who looks like an extra for Marlon Brando in *The Wild One*. No, correction. He looks like Marlon Brando in later years trying to force his way back into his costume from *The Wild One*. Talk about something your best friends won't tell you.

The guy, who is old enough to be your father — although thinking about your parents in this context kinda makes you feel faint — says something you can't make out over the music. Claude responds saucily on your behalf and drags you away, Marlon gives your ass an appreciative pat and you jump like you sat on a rocket.

"What is the *matter* with you?" Claude demands. "Behave!"

You shake your head. Claude is still hauling you along, like you're a naughty child liable to wipe your sticky fingers on the merchandise. There is a lot more leather on this side of the human barrier. Leather and sunglasses and chains. And a lot of older guys. *Old* guys.

It's hard to picture Robert here. Oh, he'd have liked the general subversive kinkiness of it, but Robert was not a kind or tolerant person when it came to other people's vulnerabilities, and you see a lot of vulnerability. A lot of soft underbelly, both figuratively and literally.

You rock to a stop, bringing Claude to a halt.

"What are we doing here?" you ask in response to his questioning look.

"We're detecting!"

"What are we detecting?"

He smiles coquettishly and nods at a blond twink in jeans and a black leather vest. "I can't speak for you, *mon cher*, but I detect *that!*"

You roll your eyes. "I'm going to investigate the bar."

You knew from the moment Claude suggested it, that this night was a waste of time and money. You turn away, but a hand hooks around your arm. You look up and your heart jumps in your chest. Detective Riordan gazes down at you with a strange half smile.

"Why, look who's here," he says in that voice that always feels like fingernails raking the back of your neck.

"Oh. Hey," you say weakly. It really IS him. Detective Riordan is in a leather club. Detective Riordan is apparently gay. Or maybe he's undercover? Then you remember the scene in Robert's apartment.

Detective Riordan was not giving you mouth-to-mouth resuscitation this afternoon, he was *kissing* you.

Your gaze falls and you take him in, from the gleam of his black boots...leather jeans...studded leather belt... and then bare, broad muscular chest. Nothing else. Not a single extra anything. Severe and elegant. Beneath the gold dusting of chest hair, his pecs look like rocks. So do his biceps. He's got an abdomen like a washboard. You can't stop staring. Your mouth is dry, your heart racketing around your chest.

"Come here often?" He's laughing at you. Well, the line of his mouth is serious enough, but his eyes glitter with amusement. Amusement and...excitement.

He wants you.

Holy moly. Detective Riordan *wants* you.

"It's my first time," you joke. "So be gentle." At least... you thought you were joking. Maybe not so much.

He blinks. Then his eyes widen.

Anyway, to make a long story short, it's true what the American Express advertising says. Membership does have its privileges. Before you can say "second thoughts," you're in a small, private room marked MEMBERS ONLY. The "members" thing makes you want to giggle, but that's because you're strung so tight with nerves you're ready to blow apart.

How can you be so anxious and so turned on all at the same time?

The room is more like a dentist's office than a bedroom, but then you're not there to sleep. There is a long — two-way?! — mirror down the length of one brick wall. There is a battered-looking armoire. Or maybe it's an entertainment console. Are you going to be filmed?

Recorded? Blackmailed? There are a couple of padded benches. Padded walls might be more appropriate. There is also a half table with a frame that looks like a cross between a rack and a baby swing. You definitely do *not* want to know.

The room is warm and the lights are low. The thump of the bass from the dance floor is like a drugged heartbeat beneath your feet.

"Do you have a safe word?"

You try not to start. Riordan is right behind you, breathing down your neck. Your scalp prickles. Your prick prickles. Your prickles prickle.

"Stop?" you offer.

"You do know how this works, right?"

"Of course," you lie.

"You need to pick a different safe word."

"Why wouldn't *stop* work? If I say stop, believe me, I mean stop."

He is not amused. "Pick another word."

"Periwinkle."

"Periwinkle it is. Now take your clothes off, Adrien," Riordan orders in a silky voice.

"Oh, right." You slowly pull your black turtleneck over your head. A black turtleneck. You're dressed more like a cat burglar than a guy hoping for some action. You fold your pullover and then don't know what to do with it. You hold it to your chest, in ingénue fashion.

Riordan observes your dilemma. His mouth quirks. "Maybe you better tell me about this fantasy of yours," he says, breaking character for a moment. Or maybe this is his character. Superior, indulgent, completely in control.

"Um, well, the usual thing," you say vaguely. How far are you going to take this? You're not sure.

"Sir."

"Sorry?"

"You address me as 'sir.'"

"Right. Sir." You almost snort, but catch yourself in time. Or do you? Riordan's mouth quirks again.

He reaches out and his fingers brush the pulse point at the base of your throat. Your heartbeat bangs away like a little blue hammer. "Why are you really here, Adrien? Don't lie to me."

Now here's a crazy thing. You open your mouth to lie to him, and you find you can't.

You swallow hard. "Robert used to come here sometimes," you admit. "Claude and I thought..." You don't finish it because it occurs to you, too late, that Riordan is not a tourist like yourself. He might have run into Robert at this club. He might be a suspect in Robert's death himself.

You stare at him wordlessly, the pulse fluttering away in the hollow of your throat. Your skin seems to tingle beneath his touch. He stares at you, and you know he can read your thoughts as easily as if they were subtitles at the bottom of a movie screen. In this case, probably a horror movie.

"Go home, Adrien-with-an-e," Riordan says softly. His breath is warm against your face, and scented of spearmint. "Go home before you get into real trouble."

If you choose to go home,
turn to page 173

If you decide to stay and get into real trouble,
turn to page 194

It occurs to you that you do know someone who was around at that time. Tara. You phone her and ask her what happened with the Chess Club. She refers you to Mr. Atkins, the sponsor of the club.

You're about to call and arrange a meeting with Mr. Atkins when Detective Riordan calls.

"We just got the paperwork from Buffalo PD. Richard Corday died from injuries sustained falling twelve stories onto a cement pool yard."

You are almost afraid to ask. "Was it suicide?"

"It was a suspicious death."

"Was there a chess piece anywhere?"

"One chess piece. A queen."

So...that's pretty conclusive, right? But Riordan seems to think there's still more investigating ahead. And, of course, it's true that your suspect has no name or face.

That evening you meet Bruce for dinner. Bruce is a nice guy, but TMI over the swordfish and fennel salad. However, you drink a bit too much, as per usual, and you don't want to spend the night alone, so you let him persuade you to go back to his place.

Bruce lives in one of those weirdly familiar Chatsworth neighborhoods, in one of those sprawling brown-and-yellow ranch-style houses. You have a little more to drink because you know in your heart you should not be leading this guy on. You have sex with Bruce and he tells you he loves you.

Oh you GUY!

When you finally drag yourself home, you find your answering machine blinking with a message from Riordan, ordering you to call the minute you get in.

Which you don't do because you don't like being ordered around (something he should know about you up front) and because you're still embarrassed your mom lodged a formal complaint about the police being too mean to you.

The next day, Mr. Atkins calls and you go meet him at the nearest Denny's.

Atkins orders the Deli Dinger and you go for the Moons Over My Hammy. Well, maybe not, but remember that old Denny's menu? That was some yummy stuff. Anyway, Atkins reveals that there was a scandal revolving around the old Chess Club. This is all news to you because you were stuck doing the whole invalid gig your junior year of high school.

"We were invited to the All City Tournament, and Grant Landis, the big doofus, cheated. Tried to cheat anyway. Knocked the board after making an illegal move or some such crap. You can't cheat at chess. Not like that."

You're full of questions. "And you quit sponsoring the club? Why not just throw Landis out? What happened to Landis? I don't remember him my senior year."

"About a month after the whole fiasco, Landis was jumped one night coming home from the library. They held him down, shaved his entire body, smeared makeup all over his face, and put him in a dress. Then the little shits took photos which they handed around the school."

"Landis must have known who did it," you point out.

"He said they wore masks. Maybe they did, but I always thought he was lying. I think he knew who it was, but what the hell. It wouldn't have made his life any easier to finger them." He adds caustically, "Nowadays, he'd have just come back with an automatic weapon."

"Why did you assume it was somebody in the Chess Club? It sounds more like something a bunch of asshole jocks would do."

"The Chess Club *was* a bunch of asshole jocks," Mr. Atkins retorts. "Hersey was on the tennis team. So were you for that matter. Felicity, or whatever her name was, was the shining star of women's softball. And Andrew Chin was a diver."

You're pretty sure that you now know who is behind Robert's murder and the attempts to terrorize you, but Mr. Atkins shoots your theory down before it even leaves the airfield.

"The one with the — er — motive would be Landis. Right? Well Landis is dead. He died right after high school."

So there goes that theory.

When you get home, Bruce has left a message wanting to get together with you AGAIN. Who knew you were so damned charming?

Detective Riordan has also left a message ordering — there's that word again — you to call him pronto.

You call Riordan rather than Bruce, which almost certainly means something. It's not even a choice because between Bruce and Riordan, there really isn't a choice.

It turns out Riordan actually has been following up on the leads you gave him, and they are heading in a direction that even he finds unsettling. "Listen," he tells you very quietly. "I don't want you to overreact, but I think you may be…next."

When you calm down enough that he can get a word in edgewise, he says, "It's this frigging Chess Club thing. I spent the last forty-eight hours checking into it."

"And?"

"They're all dead."

You stammer, "A-a-all of them? They're *all* dead?"

"All but you, buddy boy."

You share what you learned from Mr. Atkins. Riordan hears you out.

"Not too bad for an amateur, English. I'll give you that. Now listen to me very carefully. I will take it from here. You keep your goddamned nose out of it. Is that clear? Do I make myself understood?"

"And how am I supposed to protect myself?" you ask, reasonably, it seems to you.

"By letting the police do their job."

You're a little testy on this point. "Twenty-four hours ago the police thought I was a hysterical faggot making this up, if not actually a murderer. Sorry if I don't have a lot of faith in the p —"

He interrupts, "I said I was sorry. Okay? That's a murder investigation. Feelings get hurt. Hell, why am I explaining?"

He keeps explaining though, and the gist of it is, everybody's dead except you and he doesn't have a suspect. By process of elimination, YOU remain the police's favorite suspect.

Riordan's plan, such as it is, is that he will continue to follow leads and investigate, and you will stop amateur sleuthing and try to avoid getting yourself killed.

It's not much of a plan, but it's more than you got.

So you spend the rest of the evening worrying uselessly and then Bruce calls to get together.

If you choose to get together with Bruce,
turn to page 180

If you choose to listen to Riordan and stay home,
turn to page 181

If you'd like to take another look at the picture of
Adrien and Jake at Ball and Chain,
turn to page 108

You stare at Riordan for a long moment, and then, without speaking, you drag your turtleneck back on. You tell yourself you're relieved. You are way out of your element and the whole sex club thing is just...awkward. But the fact is, you feel sort of let down. Disappointed. Very disappointed.

"Hey," he says.

You look at him mutely.

"Another time." His big hand closes on the back of your neck, drawing you in. He cups the base of your skull, tilting your mouth up. He kisses you with a deep and dizzying thoroughness. Not like earlier. Not like when he was sort of giving you mouth-to-mouth resuscitation. This is very different. No one has ever kissed you like this, kissed you so hotly, so sweetly, so passionately. This is the kind of kiss they talk about in books. Well, not the books *you* read, because you read mysteries, and love — let alone sex — is a no-no in crime fiction, but you happen to know that in romance novels people kiss and the earth moves beneath their feet. Like now. You instinctively reach for Riordan because you honestly feel like the earth is slipping out from under you.

How does someone learn to kiss like that?

A *lot* of practice.

Or maybe he plays the clarinet.

At last Riordan releases you. You stagger back and he steadies you, warm hands resting on your shoulders. He's smiling. It's a knowing kind of smile. He knows exactly what that kiss does to people. That smugness is a wake-up call.

You say, with only a touch of breathlessness, "Right. Well...see you around."

His eyes narrow.

You reach behind you for the door and step out into the hall. The door swings shut, closing off your last glimpse of Riordan. He's frowning.

All around you guys are giving or getting blow jobs. Right here, in this drafty, gloomy hallway that looks like it hasn't been properly mopped since...since the last time the Bacchanalia held their quarterly shareholders meeting. Nothing like a little public sex to break the magic spell. There but for the grace of God...

You return to the main floor of the club and look for Claude.

He's nowhere to be found.

You try calling him on your cell phone, but he doesn't pick up.

Finally you notice Riordan has also returned to the main room and is zeroing in on a slender, red-haired man about your own age. You definitely don't want to be around to watch that merger go through.

You head for the main entrance and as you exit, a fire alarm goes off.

People start piling out of the club, and you spot Claude. He is holding his embroidered leather pants up with one hand and holding his keys with the other.

"Why didn't you answer your phone? Where have you been?" you demand.

"The same place as you," he pants.

"I don't think so!"

"Not the same *pants*," he says. "The same place. The Members Only part of the club."

"Wait a minute. Are you telling me you're a member?"

"Did I say that?"

"Are you telling me that skinny little twink —?"

Claude grabs you, turning you toward the parking lot. "Will you let it go? Let's get out of here."

You run for the parking lot, jostling shoulders with the people running around you. "I thought we were supposed to be investigating Robert's murder?" you continue to bitch. "You just brought me here so you could get laid."

"I brought you here so you could get laid," Claude retorts. "I've never seen anyone who needs to get laid more than you, *ma belle*."

There should be a special ring in hell reserved for helpful friends.

Claude drives you home and you wish him sweet dreams. Surely there's some country where that gesture means "sweet dreams"? I mean, if the peace sign can also mean V for Victory...

Anyway, you bid Claude a fond adieu and head upstairs to get plastered. You're on your third brandy when the downstairs buzzer rings.

You're not expecting anyone.

The memory of Rob's gruesome death rises spectral-like before you.

Warily, you sneak downstairs, not turning on the shop lights, and peer outside.

Moonlight — er, no — streetlight illumines the pale hair and flinty profile of Detective Riordan. His dark gaze probes past the glass door and security gate, though it's doubtful you're more than a shadow in the dim interior. He rings the buzzer again.

The sound is jarringly loud in the silent building.

Is this how Robert met his fate? You'd have to be crazy to open the door to Riordan. You know for sure now he's a suspect in Robert's murder, right?

Of course, so are you.

You continue to watch him. He's wearing a black leather coat over his leather jeans. Is he still bare-chested beneath that coat? Does he still have that belt with the studs on? Aren't police officers always supposed to be armed? Where the hell would he hide a gun in that outfit?

As you stand there weighing the pros and cons, he reaches up and gives the back of his neck a squeeze like his muscles are tight or he's nervous.

The gesture disarms you.

If you choose to let Riordan in,
turn to page 220

If you choose to sneak up the stairs and pretend you
never heard the buzzer,
turn to page 187

If you can't quite decide, turn to page 9

You order Chinese takeout and then you take another look at that yearbook of Rob's. It occurs to you that you do know someone who was around at that time. Tara. You phone her and ask her what happened with the Chess Club. She refers you to Mr. Atkins, the sponsor of the club.

You arrange to meet with Mr. Atkins the following afternoon.

Detective Riordan calls. "We just got the paperwork from Buffalo PD. Richard Corday died from injuries sustained falling twelve stories onto a cement pool yard."

"You are almost afraid to ask. "Was it suicide?"

"It was a suspicious death."

"Was there a chess piece anywhere?"

"One chess piece. A queen."

So...that's pretty conclusive, right? But Riordan seems to think there's still more investigating ahead. And, of course, it's true that your suspect has no name or face.

Riordan also says that Tara was in Los Angeles around the time of Robert's death, which you didn't know. Of course, if Robert is the victim of a serial killer, that lets Tara out.

After Riordan hangs up, you watch a little TV. A local channel is running a late night marathon of an old British cop show called *The Professionals*.

You watch a couple of episodes, then you turn the TV off, brush your teeth and go to bed. You dream you're driving around Los Angeles in a gold Capri while being chased by terrorists. The terrorists all have wax vampire fangs like the ones you used to be able to get for Halloween. (Maybe you can still get them, but it's a long time since you've gone trick or treating.)

Anyway, the terrorists hurl death threats at you, but the fear factor is significantly undermined by the fact that they have to keep sucking up their drool thanks to the wax teeth.

So that's that. Not that I want to judge anyone's choices, but you probably should have gone to dinner with Bruce.

If you choose to return to the main storyline,
turn to page 171

Or if you're feeling lucky,
just turn to a random page.

If you choose to get together with Bruce,
turn to page 180

WHY ARE YOU ALWAYS CHOOSING TO GET TOGETHER WITH BRUCE?

That's the question you should be asking yourself.

Personally, I think getting together with Bruce again is just kind of boring. How about a three-way with Kit Holmes and J.X. Moriarity instead?

Yeah, I thought you'd like that.

PSYCH.

Unfortunately Kit Holmes is pretty adamant that he will not be part of any threesome. He's still struggling with the idea of being part of a twosome.

My best suggestion? Turn to page 37

Or you could always return to the safety of page 178

"Where have you been all day? Why didn't you call?" Bruce demands first thing, which is not an auspicious opening.

You bring Bruce up to speed as much as you can — in other words, you totally lie to him about what you've been doing all day.

"Let me come over."

"Not tonight." You try to soften it. "I'm going to have an early night."

Bruce doesn't take rejection well. "Why don't you just say what you mean?"

"I'm trying to," you say. This is why you don't date a lot.

Bruce keeps on. "If I was the right person, you wouldn't want time or space. You'd want to be with me like I want to be with you."

He's probably right. "Bruce, don't back me into a corner. It's just one night."

"That's what you think."

Self-fulfilling prophecy, but you're too tactful to point that out. To your relief, Bruce hangs up on you and you spend the evening getting — surprise! — sloshed.

When you wake from your drunken stupor a couple of hours later, it's to the jingle jangle of another of those heavy breathing anonymous phone calls you've been getting lately.

"Adrien..." A hoarse whisper that, despite common sense, starts your heart stuttering and stammering in your chest. "Adrien. I'm going to kill you."

The caller hangs up.

You dial *69. The phone rings and rings and then...

"Hello?" Bruce asks doubtfully.

You hang up.

If you choose to call Detective Riordan,
turn to page 188

If you choose to —
CRAP!!! THE PHONE IS RINGING AGAIN!!!
Turn the page!

The phone is still ringing.

Your hand reaches out and you pick up the handset. You listen.

Silence.

"Bruce?" you whisper.

"Adrien?" Bruce says at once.

You know he's working through the last five minutes, wondering whether you know the truth, wondering how you could possibly not know the truth...

But the one thing you have going in your favor is the fact that Bruce wants to believe with all his heart that you really don't have a clue. You just have to play along and he'll do all the heavy lifting.

Or so you hope.

You falter, "I-I hoped it was you. You're right. I don't want to be alone tonight."

You can hear the confusion and wariness in his silence. He says finally, "What's happened?"

You babble some ridiculous story only a lunatic would believe. Oh right. Target audience.

"I'm on my way."

You call Riordan at work and then you call him at his home number. You leave a message. "It's Adrien English," you say. "My friend Bruce just called. Bruce Green, the reporter. I think he may have...may be..." Yeah, no wonder you're a writer. You have such a way with words. "I'm going over to his house. Unless I hear from you first." You don't remember the house address, but you tell Riordan the street and what the house looked like. "It's nine-thirty."

You forget to mention that Bruce is on his way to the bookstore, but maybe that's a good reason for you high-tailing it out of there because otherwise this is NOT a good adventure to choose.

But you've been dating Bruce, you feel like you owe him this.

The road to Hell is paved with good intentions.

If you really do choose to go to Bruce's house,
turn to page 185

If you change your mind and decide to wait
at the bookstore for Bruce and/or Riordan,
turn to page 190

Bruce's house is dark but the porch light shines welcomingly as you walk up the front drive. You unlatch the side gate and sneak around the back.

You take out your pocket knife and start prying at the screen fastenings of Bruce's bedroom window. This would probably be a dream come true for him if he was home, but he's not. He's probably knocking on your front door right now, so you'd better hurry the hell up before he figures out what's going on.

You're lifting the screen out of the frame when a hand clamps onto your shoulder. Before you can scream — er, shout in a manly fashion — for help, another hand clamps over your mouth. You struggle, and then a familiar voice hisses, "Knock it off!"

Luckily, it's Riordan-familiar and not Bruce-familiar.

A few moments of disheartening, but not unexpected, misunderstanding occur. Riordan thinks your actions seem kinda suspicion, all things considered. Finally, you manage to convince him that you're merely nuts (and a little drunk), not homicidal.

You share your suspicions of Bruce.

Riordan is ahead of you this time. "This is where Grant Landis lived growing up. This is the house he supposedly died in."

"Supposedly?"

186

"Landis isn't dead. There's no death certificate."

"But..." You're very much afraid you know what's coming.

"Bruce *is* Landis. Until six years ago, Bruce Green didn't exist. No DMV records, no TRW report — there's no trace of him before that." Riordan grabs you and hauls you toward the side gate. That grip is going to leave bruises. "I asked you to stay out of it. I specifically told you. What do I have to do? Arrest you?"

"Anything to get me in handcuffs?"

Probably not the time, but yeah, there's something going on between you two.

You agree to go swear out a complaint against Green, which is probably Riordan's way of getting you safely into police custody, and you start back for your car.

You're too late. Bruce is pulling up just as you're crossing the street.

If you choose to run for your car,
turn to page 199

If you choose to stop and talk to Bruce,
turn to page 201

Really?

The End

You phone Detective Riordan at police headquarters, or whatever it's properly called, but you're told he's left for the day.

You didn't really think just because a psychopath is planning your imminent grisly murder, Riordan was working on your case 24/7, did you?

He needs his dinner!

He needs his rest.

He needs time to take red-headed girls on dates!

You try the other phone numbers he left when he called the night you and Bruce went to dinner another lifetime ago.

Riordan doesn't pick up, though there is an answering machine on at what is presumably his home number.

It's not really an easy situation to describe on a few seconds of tape, so you hang up without leaving a message.

After all, just because Bruce is stalking you and leaving creepy messages it doesn't automatically mean he's a murderer. He might just be…well…emotionally arrested. He might be disturbed. Who isn't these days? It needn't follow that he's dangerous.

Come to think of it, this is why you're hesitant to get romantically involved again. There's nothing like love to drive otherwise normal people to acts of madness.

You replace the receiver and pace up and down your living room. The phone begins to ring again.

If you choose to answer the phone,
turn to page 183

If you choose to flee into the night,
turn to page 234.

Naturally, you're a nervous wreck while you wait for Bruce — or Riordan — to show up. Mostly because the chances of Riordan showing up seem pretty slim, and the chances of Bruce showing up seem all too likely.

Should you call the police again? It's going to be embarrassing, but isn't that better than being dead?

The problem is, you don't know for sure that Bruce *is* a killer. It's still pretty hard to believe. And it's already hurtful enough to break up with someone without accusing them of being a serial killer.

You're still undecided, still pacing up and down the bookshop floor, when Bruce arrives. He knocks on the glass door at the front entrance, and you let him in.

He tries to take you in his arms, not seeming to notice that you're stiff as a board in his arms. "I'm glad you called me," he says.

"I'm glad you came," you lie.

"Did something happen?" He's watching you with an almost eager light in his eyes.

Is it possible he wants a confrontation? You just don't know. You don't want to know, that's the truth.

"I think I'm being stalked," you tell him.

He continues to watch you in that odd, alert way. "Oh?" he says finally.

You nod.

"By who?" he asks eventually, when you don't offer further information.

You open your mouth, but the words won't come.

Observing your struggle, Bruce suddenly smiles. It's a horrible smile because he isn't Bruce anymore. He's a stranger. He's the man who killed Robert and Claude and is going to do his best to kill you.

"That didn't take you as long as I expected," he remarks and lunges for you.

You dodge him, ducking behind the nearest bookshelf. The shop is a rabbit warren of tall shelves and you know the floor plan well. You move quietly down the aisles, watching and listening for Bruce.

You have three potential escape routes: the stairs to your apartment, the front entrance, which you left unlocked in case Riordan does show up, and the side door which is locked — but it won't take long to throw a deadbolt.

The side door leaves you out in a deserted alley and the front door leaves you out on the deserted sidewalk of a part of town which is closed up at this time of night. Your instinct is to head for the safety of your own living quarters, but not only does it sound like Bruce is lurking in that general area — probably guessing the direction of your thoughts — if you get cornered upstairs, you're out of options.

No wait. There's a fourth option. If you can get into your office, you can lock the door and use the phone there to call the police. You can even use some of the storage boxes and shelves to barricade yourself in.

You wait, listening. You stay absolutely motionless, barely breathing. When you hear a book fall over to your left, you make a dash for your office.

Too late, you realize Bruce is smarter than you thought. He must have picked up a paperback from the sales counter and thrown it to make you think he was coming up on your left. In fact, he's standing in front of you, blocking your access to the office.

You veer right and run for the staircase. You're four steps up before he grabs you and throws you bodily down the stairway. You crash-land on your back, winded and stunned. Bruce looms over you and you see he's holding a huge hunting knife. Has he been carrying that the whole time?

You roll away, knowing it's too late.

But no. A sudden commotion — someone is blowing a whistle at the top of their lungs, the shrill sound filling the night — and rescue comes from out of left field. An elderly man is beating Bruce with a poker — your poker — and a woman with dark, frizzy hair is wailing away at Bruce with her shoulder bag while still blowing frantically on her whistle.

You crawl out of range, scramble to your feet, steadying yourself on the wooden counter. Your saviors have knocked Bruce to his knees. He drops his knife and covers his head.

You retrieve the knife. You manage to stop the elderly man and dark-haired woman from killing Bruce.

You tie Bruce up and the three of you wait for the police.

It turns out that the elderly man is Henry Harrison, the very same old guy who turned up with that bus tour the morning after Robert was murdered. You found him snooping around your living room, remember? The woman is named Janet Blimes. She's Henry's neighbor. That's their story anyway.

Henry and Janet reveal that they've been hunting for something called The Cross of Rouen which they believe is hidden somewhere in the bookstore.

It's a little convoluted, to say the least, but the important thing is, thanks to their attempt to break into your place of business, Henry and Janet saved your life.

By the time Riordan and the police show up, you and Henry and Janet are on your second brandies and well on your way to becoming lifelong friends. They even promise to cut you in on the reward if you help them find the lost artifact.

The End

"**G**o home, Adrien-with-an-e," Riordan says softly. His breath is warm against your face, and scented of spearmint. "Go home before you get into real trouble."

"Trouble is my business," you say. An idiotic comment, unless you're Phillip Marlowe, but then this whole setup is so artificial, so stagy. Except Riordan. Riordan is the real deal.

"Is that so?" He's got a little growl in his voice which is sort of alarming and sort of a turn-on all at the same time. He bumps your face with his. You step back and he does it again, crowding in on you until your back is against the door.

"This is a good way to lose an antler," you say, and then you're out of words — and breath — because his lips are parting yours, and his tongue is insinuating its way into your mouth before you can say French kiss. Or even *Mon Dieu!*

Being rather reserved, you're not all that keen on having a mere acquaintance shove one of his organs down your throat, but Riordan is surprisingly sophisticated in his approach. His tongue twines with yours, he nibbles your mouth, and sucks on your tongue. It's unexpectedly hot, and if you hadn't been turned on before, you would be now.

He shoves an aggressive knee between your legs and rests his forearms on either side of your head. You're effectively trapped as he rubs himself against you like the big horny animal he is. And that's okay by you. You moan into his mouth and grind your crotch against Riordan's fierce bulge. In a minute you're going to be whimpering for him to take you, but then that's the idea of a place like this right?

Riordan reaches down, fastens his hand on your waistband and rips your jeans open. Yes. *Rips.* You hear denim tear and the metal rivet bounce off one of the padded benches. Okay, it's just the threads holding the button, but still. You do whimper at that display of power, arching into his bigger, stronger body. It's crazy and primal, but you need him to fuck you. Need it now...

So it is with something like horror that you hear a fire alarm ringing on the other side of the wall.

Riordan goes rigid — the other kind of rigid — and the small sound of frustration he makes isn't far from your own earlier noises. His mouth parts from yours, and you sag against the door. He is breathing equally hard.

You say, "I don't..."

"Fucking believe it," he finishes.

You gaze at each other in disbelief, waiting for the alarm to stop, but it doesn't stop. In fact, you can now hear people filling the hallway outside of the room, moving toward the back entrance of the building.

You start to laugh. After a frowning moment, Riordan's face changes and he starts to laugh as well. He throws you your shirt and you pull it on. You have to hold your jeans closed as he opens the door.

Riordan leads the way down the hall and out the back of the building. The parking lot is crowded with people in various states of disrobe, and though there is no sign of smoke, you can hear sirens in the distance.

So can Riordan. He says, "Did you want to get out of here?"

Yes. You want it so much you don't trust your voice.

You follow Riordan to his home in Glendale. It's a nice little house on a quiet residential street. Little do the neighbors know what that nice police officer next door gets up to.

He throws his dog in the backyard and you find yourself slammed down on the kitchen table, jeans around your ankles, being thoroughly fucked.

It's fast and furious and all you can do is hang onto the table and ride out those strong, teeth-jarring thrusts. Your own stiff cock bobs painfully against the rounded edge of the table. Your gaze is fastened on a stack of unopened mail. There's an Auto Club magazine on top and you can't seem to look away from the scene of palm trees wrapped in Christmas lights.

"Oh yeah," Riordan mutters. "You're a born bottom, baby. You're made for this."

Not really. Not usually. But tonight, yeah. Something strange is happening here tonight and all you can do is grip the sides of the table and beg for more. "God. Oh God. Please...Harder..."

The feel of that thick, hot shaft moving inside you. A pass over your prostate sends a charge of electricity crackling up your spine and short circuits your brain. Christmas lights scintillate behind your eyelids. You're going to be drooling on the wooden table top in a second.

The table scoots a few inches forward as Riordan continues to pound your ass. *Oh yeah.* Right there...

"Tell me what you want?" Riordan breathlessly demands, and you obediently spill out an inarticulate jumble of pleading and gratitude for what he's doing to you — and what he's going to do to you any second.

And there it is. The thrill at the base of your cock, the tingle in your belly. Your balls pull up tight. Riordan groans, his hips still, and he empties into you.

Did you really just engage in unprotected sex with Detective Riordan on his kitchen table?

Yeah, you did, and far from turning you off, you start to come yourself. Distantly you wonder whether you're going to have to eat breakfast at that table sometime in the future...

You do end up having breakfast at that same table. Riordan invites you to stay the night, which you do. It's surprisingly nice being with him even when you're not having sex. In the morning, he fucks you again — in bed this time — and afterwards fixes you scrambled eggs and toast.

You're eating breakfast when his girlfriend shows up unannounced. It is not a pleasant scene, but afterwards, Riordan seems both depressed and relieved. He says he would like to see you again, and you say it can probably be arranged.

You drive home to Pasadena and discover Cloak and Dagger books has burnt to the ground. The arson inspector is on the scene and he informs you the suspected arsonist perished in the flames.

You can't help wishing Detective Riordan had not ruined your only surviving pair of jeans.

The End

Please tell me you're not going to try and outrun a car?

Okay. You take off running.

You're actually pretty fast on your feet, and your strategy catches Bruce by surprise, so you get a few yards safe distance before he slams down on the accelerator and speeds after you.

You know before you reach the Bronco that you won't be able to get the door open in time, so you veer right, cross the sidewalk, and jump over the nearest white picket fence, sprinting for the front porch of a nearby house.

As you peel off, you see a figure come racing out of the bushes on the left side of the street. Riordan opens fire on Bruce.

Bruce loses control of his car and crashes into your Bronco. The airbags in both cars deploy.

Riordan, gun trained on Bruce's motionless form, warily approaches the crashed vehicle. He reaches inside. After a moment he steps back, looks at you, and shakes his head.

Poor crazy Bruce.

Detective Riordan gets a medal for saving your life, and you eventually become friends. He's actually not such a bad guy when you get to know him.

He even invites you to his wedding to police woman Kate Keegan. It's a lovely wedding. You bring Mel, who's in town visiting his parents.

The End

"**W**hat are you doing here?" Bruce calls to you. "I went to your place."

"I-I thought we decided to meet here," you call back.

"No. I said I would come to you."

"I was too jumpy to wait. I'm...uh...I'm afraid I'm being watched."

"By the police?"

"No. Yes. I don't know." Baby, you're a natural at this!

"What did you park down here for?" You can hear the frown in Bruce's voice.

"I'm not thinking clearly," you answer. "I'm afraid."

"Of what?"

Of you. You're not sure you can make it across the street, unlock the Bronco and get in before he overtakes you. You could start yelling for Riordan, but would he hear you this far down the block?

Anyway, the bottom line is you need proof. That's why you came here in the first place.

You shiver and say, "Are we going to stand out here talking all night?"

Bruce reaches across and unlocks the door. "Get in."

If you choose to run for your car,
turn to page 202

If you choose to get in the car with Bruce,
turn to page 206

Didn't you just try this?

You sprint for your car.

Behind you, Bruce guns the motor and screeches after you.

Your feet pound the pavement and you swerve, running for the sidewalk lined with trees, but you're crazy if you think you can outrun a car.

Then again, you probably *are* crazy or you wouldn't have gotten yourself in this jam. This kind of thing doesn't happen to Christopher Holmes, if you'll notice.

You feel the heat from the engine against your back, and you zig left and sharply reverse, a move you perfected playing tennis many years ago.

Bruce hauls on the steering wheel and the car skids, careening across the residential street. Lights are going on in the houses, and you see a figure race out of the shadows. The street lamps turn his hair silver, gleam on the gun he's aiming at the car skidding toward him.

He fires. Three shots. The sound is shockingly loud as the echo seems to bounce off the tidy houses and neat fences.

Two bullets blast the windshield of Bruce's car, but the car hurtles on. The third bullet slams into the engine block. Riordan leaps away, though the car bumper delivers him a glancing blow. He tumbles onto the grass. The car plows into one of the trees, hood crumpling accordion-style. You see the airbag deploy like a mushroom cloud. The car horn is blaring deafeningly. Leaves and twigs drift down in a green shower, gilded by lamplight.

You run past the car to Riordan. He's lying face down and your heart stops.

"Riordan? Detective?"

He lifts his head and swears faintly. You drop down beside him. "Don't try to move."

"Where's Landis?" he asks. You can just make the words out over the bray of the horn.

You look at the car. Steam rises from under the hood. The deployed air bag has already wilted away, but you can't see Bruce behind the cobweb of broken glass. There's no motion from inside the car.

All up and down the street, doors are opening and people are cautiously stepping outside.

"Call 911," you yell. To Riordan, you say, "I don't think he's moving."

"Make. Sure."

You jump up and go over to the car. Bruce is slumped over on his side. He's clearly dead, and you turn away shuddering.

Poor crazy bastard.

You go sit with Riordan who, despite his efforts to remain stoic, is clearly in a lot of pain.

"Just hang on," you tell Riordan. "You're going to be okay." You have no idea whether that's true or not. You take his cold hand in yours because if it was you in his place — and it nearly was — you'd like to know you weren't alone. "Thank you," you tell him.

He squeezes your hand weakly.

More cops arrive, and then the ambulance finally shows up. Riordan gets hauled off to the hospital. You try calling a few times, and finally you're told that he's in stable condition and can even have visitors.

You buy a fruit basket and head over to the hospital. But when you finally track down Riordan's room, he's already got a visitor. A pretty red-haired woman in a police uniform. Riordan is sitting up in bed and he looks pretty healthy despite having a leg in traction. He seems in pretty good spirits, laughing at something the woman is saying.

You try to duck out without being seen, but no such luck. The police woman spots you and before you can say Awkward Situation, you've been ushered into the room, still clutching your fruit basket. After the first startled look of recognition, Riordan seems unable to meet your eyes.

The police woman introduces herself as Kate Keegan, Riordan's fiancée. You hand her the fruit basket as a consolation prize, thank Riordan again for saving your life, and bid them both farewell.

You stop off on your way home to stock up on Tab and Ramen soup.

Maybe you should get a cat. They say every bookstore needs a cat.

The End

You get in the car with Bruce. He drives you up the street and parks in the garage. You get out and go inside the house.

What choice do you have? You don't know if Riordan sees what's happening or not. What will he do? What does he expect you to do?

What you do is undress and go to bed with Bruce. You try to claim that your heart is bothering you, but he's not in a sympathetic mood. He gives you wine and then fucks you. In a weird way that seems fair to you, given that you're fucking him over.

Of course, the difference is Bruce is a homicidal nut job and you're just running out of options.

You keep reminding yourself that it's just sex. Harsh, unhappy sex, but it won't kill you. Bruce gulps hotly in your ear, he's leaving bruises either by accident or intent, and all the while you're painfully conscious that Riordan may be outside the window watching or listening. Embarrassing though that would be, it would also be a comfort. You have never felt lonelier in your life than lying beneath Bruce.

Finally, Bruce falls asleep on top of you. Eventually, you get the nerve up to move. You start for the door, and you spot Riordan down the hall. He's holding a very large gun and he does *not* seem happy to see you. He gestures for you to get the hell out.

You want to.

You want nothing more than that.

But Bruce is already sitting up, speaking to you. "What are you looking for? Come back to bed."

You say, "It's late. I should go." Which is perfectly true.

"Come back to bed, Adrien."

If you choose to run for it,
turn to page 208

If you choose to get back in bed with Bruce,
turn to page 213

Congratulations! Any sane, sensible person would run for it.

You throw a quick look back at Bruce. Even in the dark he can read your intention. He lunges off the bed. He's coming for you.

Shit! He's fast.

You twist away from him and sprint down the hall toward Riordan, your heart thundering in your ears like a herd of buffalo stampeding across the Plains. Or maybe that pounding is the sound of Bruce's feet as he comes up behind you again.

Jesus, this is the longest hallway ever built. It should be in the Guinness Book of Records.

"Drop," Riordan yells.

At least that's what you hope he said. Maybe what he said was, "Drop it!"

But you're going with your instinct, and that is to get out of the line of fire. As you dive for the floor, you see the muzzle flash, feel the singe as a warm blast parts your hair, and then you slam down on the dusty floor.

Three shots, one after another, the bangs seeming to collide, crashing into each other, reverberating off the wood floor and plaster walls.

You lie there for a moment, stunned, winded.

Riordan is walking toward you, pistol trained on whatever is dragging in those agonized, ragged breaths behind you.

He's saying something. It takes you a second to understand the words.

"This way, baby. Keep moving toward me." You start to push up and he says in what seems to be a ridiculously calm voice, "Keep left. Don't get in front of the gun."

You duck down again, and flatten yourself to the wall. You can't look around. What is the matter with you that you can't look at Bruce?

"Are you hurt? Are you injured?" Riordan is not looking at you, so it takes you a second to realize he means you.

"I'm okay."

"You sure?"

He stops beside you, though his attention — and weapon — are still trained on Bruce.

The wet gurgling sounds stop suddenly and there's a single metallic clink. You turn around then.

Bruce is sprawled against the linen cupboard at the end of the hallway. He is sitting in what looks like a pool of blood. It's hard to see in the dim light, but your eyes eventually make out that the top of his head is gone. On the floor, a knife glints in the dull light.

The silence is even more terrifying than the sounds of dying.

Riordan drops to one knee. "Look at me."

You turn to him though it is hard to get the image of Bruce with half his head blown away out of your mind.

To your shock, Riordan puts his hand on the side of your face, like he's checking your eyes for concussion. His gaze is almost piercing. "How badly did he hurt you?"

You're not even sure what he means at first. Then you remember that in some corners of the world the sex you just had with Bruce qualifies as rape. It seems both strange and touching that Riordan would recognize this before you do.

"I think I hurt him more," you say.

His thumb tracks a gentle line along your cheekbone. "Can you stand up?"

"Of course."

But the fact is, when you try to stand, you're sick and shaky and grateful for the arm Riordan puts around you. He walks you into the living room, grabs a black granny square afghan from the back of the sofa, and wraps it around you. For a minute he sits with you, his arm around your shoulders, and you lean into him grateful for the silent support.

Funny. Detective Riordan never struck you as the kind of guy anyone would turn to for comfort. You were wrong about that. You've been wrong about a lot of things. Like maybe Detective Riordan could also use some comfort. After all, he just killed a man. That has to be a new experience for him too, right? You can hear his heart banging away in the wake of all that adrenaline.

"Are *you* okay?" you ask.

He gives a funny laugh, and nods, like he doesn't trust himself to speak.

By then you notice a glittering sea of red and blue lights outside the windows. The cavalry. Better late than never.

Riordan lets go of you. He rises, goes to the front door to let in John Law, but then pauses.

"Adrien?"

You look up.

"It's liable to get rough."

You nod.

God, is this going to get in the newspapers? Is your mother going to read about it and choke to death on her Earl Grey?

"But if you need...anything..." He's giving you such an odd, intense look. That expression in his eyes. You can't tell if it's hope or fear or both.

Maybe because you're not sure whether what *you* feel is hope or fear.

You say, "I don't even know your first name."

"Jake."

"Jake. Okay, Jake. Thank you. For...everything." You give him a tentative smile.

His answering smile is equally tentative.

He turns and opens the door.

The End

You turn from the door and walk back to the bed. Gingerly, you sit on the edge.

Bruce watches your every move. He says — and there's a strange, almost cherishing note in his voice, "What's wrong?"

"Nothing."

Silence.

Then Bruce says flatly, "Oh."

And everything changes. The delicate balance both of you worked so hard to preserve, to avoid facing what you know to be true, tips.

Bruce jumps off the bed, stalks over to the bedroom door, and slams it shut. He can't know Riordan is out there waiting. Can he?

You can hear Bruce's harsh breaths in the stifling darkness. Tree branches scratch at the window. There is just enough light from the waning moon to see Bruce's silhouette by the door. He is motionless. What is he waiting for?

What are *you* waiting for?

Keep them talking, right? That's how it works on TV. "Bruce?"

You can see his shadow moving now, hear him opening a drawer. "I know, Adrien." He sounds absent, like a parent pacifying a restless child.

It's frightening not to be able to see what he's doing, to hear those furtive, rustling noises. You glimpse his reflection in the mirror, the pale glimmer of his body. He turns toward you, and in the gloom you can discern the outline of white — a grim smile that isn't Bruce. Isn't human. He's wearing a mask. A skull mask which he unhurriedly adjusts over his head.

You leap off the bed and back into the nightstand, nearly knocking the lamp off. You can still see Bruce's reflection as he continues to rummage through his drawer. What the hell is he looking for? The eyes of the askew mask stare sightlessly your way.

Light glints on silver. Bruce holds up a blade. He walks toward you, knife upheld.

You snap on the bedside lamp. Bruce freezes.

"Turn that out," he says hoarsely.

You can't seem to look away from the knife. It's huge. Sharp. A butcher's knife. You imagine it sliding into your chest.

"Bruce, why are you doing this?"

"Now *that's* a silly question."

Possibly. But you keep trying. "Bruce —"

"Don't call me that."

"What do you want me to call you? Grant? Take the mask off," you tell him. "Since we're not pretending."

Bruce begins to rant and rave. He seems to think he was on some divine mission. It's pretty confusing. You wonder what the hell Riordan is doing. Any minute now Bruce is going to lunge at you and you're going to... probably die, given the lack of room to maneuver.

You keep talking because that's all you can do now. "You think God wants you to kill people because of a high school prank?"

Bruce cries, *"Prank?* That prank destroyed my life. Ruined me. You have no idea what you're talking about!"

"So explain it to me."

His eyes study you through the eye holes in the mask. "Believe me, you won't agree with my reasoning. I've tried explaining before. How's this? Everything that has happened to me happened because of Robert Hersey and his sycophantic buddies. Everything."

"That's not reasonable, Br — Grant. You're too smart to believe —"

He interrupted casually, "But enough about me. This is about you."

"Me?"

"Yes, you. YOU, YOU, YOU!" he jabs at the air, shrieking. "You made this happen. Not me. I always liked you, even though you *never* noticed me." His hand slashes through the air. "NEVER NOTICED —"

Bruce calms again. "I tried to get all my classes with you. I used to always sit behind you. Remember? Pathetic, isn't it? You even came to this house once, you know. I couldn't believe you didn't remember."

You ask, "Did you want me to remember?"

He seemed to consider this. "When I saw you in the church I wanted to protect you from those fucking cops. But the truth is, you like those fucking cops, don't you? You like that blond one."

You would like that blond one to show up about now. That's for sure. You start edging for the door. "Tell me something. Why Claude? What did he ever do to you?"

"Who?" Bruce sounds genuinely confused. Then he explains that he killed Claude because you cancelled your date with him. That's it. That's the last straw. You break and run for the door.

Bruce gets there first. He holds the knife up but doesn't stab you. Surely it's a good sign that he wants to keep talking?

You both turn at movement outside the window. Bruce grabs you, using you as a shield as an iron lawn chair comes crashing through the bedroom window — followed by Riordan.

Riordan hits the floor in a shoulder roll and comes up on one knee, aiming his pistol at you and Bruce. Well, he's probably aiming at Bruce, but you're in the way.

You really, really do not want to be shot. Every bit as much as you don't want to be stabbed. You'd probably have a better chance of surviving being stabbed — survival rates are higher in stabbings — but even thinking about being stabbed is sending your heart into overdrive.

"Put down the knife." Riordan sounds calm and instructive.

"No! Put down the gun. I'll kill him if you don't!"

To your everlasting relief, Riordan does not behave like a cop on TV or the movies. He does not put the gun down. He blasts Bruce.

There's a big bang. Plaster peppers your face and hair. Bruce lets go of you and you stumble away in a daze. Bruce slides down the wall and falls over.

"Okay, baby?"

Riordan is talking to you. He just called you "baby." Like the two of you are cool cats in a 1960s PI flick. Or something. It's hard to think straight with Bruce gurgling his last breaths behind you.

This is terrible. Terrible.

You stare into Riordan's hazel eyes. He's still talking to you in that calm, quiet way as though he thinks you're going to lose the plot any moment. You're not going to lose the plot, but you feel kind of weird and lightheaded. And then Riordan's hand locks around the back of your neck, he draws you forward. You lean into him, and his arm goes around your waist. Your head seems to fit right in the curve of his neck and shoulder.

218

For a second or two, you hang on to each other. Riordan's heart is banging away as hard as yours. Neither of you says a word.

Then the front door crashes open and a dozen uniforms burst into the living room with weapons drawn.

A few hours later, all the questions have been asked, and you've even been able to answer some of them. Black-and-whites are angled all over the street. The Landis yard and sidewalk has been sectioned off, and a crowd is forming behind the yellow crime scene tape. Birds are starting to twitter in the trees, the street lamps are winking off.

Riordan materializes and says he's going to drive you home.

In silence, you walk down the shady street. Riordan holds his hand out and you surrender your keys. It feels, well, a little symbolic. Maybe you should have chosen to drive. Maybe not.

You look at him, at the hard line of his jaw, the severe haircut, the almost shy way his eyes flick to yours and then away. You say, "I don't know your first name."

"Jake." He does it again. Looks at you. Looks away.

Neither of you speaks as you sit in the Bronco waiting for the engine to warm. Riordan yawns so widely his jaw cracks. He scrubs his face with his hands. Gives you a sideways look. "You know, this won't be an easy thing, Adrien."

"The investigation you mean?"

"No." He gives you a funny, twisted grin. Like he thinks the joke is on him. He says softly, "No, I don't mean that."

You stare out at the first blush of sunrise lighting the surrounding Chatsworth hills. You look back at him.

He's smiling at you.

The End

What the heck. You only live once, right?

With a sense of déjà vu you shove back the ornate security gate, unlock the glass front doors, and let him in.

Riordan stares at you for a long, long moment.

You open your mouth to say something smart-assed about making house calls, but then you don't. It occurs to you that, unbelievable as it is, he's off-balance and a little uncertain. And it's not a feeling he likes.

This could go a number of ways, and not all of them pleasant.

So you tell the truth. "I've been thinking about you all night."

That must be the right thing to say because next thing you know you're in his arms and he's kissing you. When you stop for breath, he mutters, "I can't believe how much I like kissing you."

Which...is probably a compliment although it seems a little grudging.

"I like kissing you too," you offer. It's the truth. You could get used to the firm press of his warm mouth against yours.

"I want to fuck you."

"I want to fuck *you*," you say.

He goes very still.

"Just kidding," you say. Although…wow. You *would* like that. You already know, even before he backs you into a bookshelf and starts working the fastening to your jeans, that he does not negotiate on this point. And that's okay. The take charge attitude is kind of relaxing. For now.

You try to slip your arms around his neck and initiate a second kiss. He kisses you back with hungry efficiency, pulling your arms above your head and yanking your jeans down. Which takes a couple of yanks because you're skinny and you like your jeans to fit properly.

His tongue tastes warm and gingery, like he was sucking on a Red Hot or an Atomic Fireball on the drive over. He doesn't seem like the kind of guy who would have a sweet tooth, but that's kind of a snap judgment given that you barely know him. His tongue pushes against yours. He's kissing you hotly, wetly, deeply. The odd idea goes through your mind that this is his idea of a passionate kiss and maybe not natural to him. It's skillful, though. No question. Your mind is whirling by the time he's got both your cocks free.

There's a crazy *Star Wars* moment, what with the stiff and dueling light sabers and Riordan breathing in your ear like Darth Vader. He takes your cock in his hand and proceeds to pump you with strong, even strokes. It's effective, if maybe a little too workmanlike. You can't help wondering how he'd be if he was relaxed and knew you a little better, didn't feel establishing the boundaries was a priority. You'd like to keep a little corner of your brain detached and focused on business too, but it just feels too good. Even if his grip is a little tight and the pace a little too brisk.

He probably doesn't know his own strength. He's pretty damned strong — he's using his other hand to keep your arms pinned over your head. It's a tiring position, and one that emphasizes your helplessness, but when you try to lower them, he won't let you. One hand is holding you in place, one hand is working you, and all you're allowed to do is respond. Well, you could kick him, but if you're honest, you don't want to interrupt the rhythm because that delightfully familiar curl of pleasure — too keen for such an ordinary word as "pleasure" — is starting to unwind and spiral deep inside you.

"I'm going to come," you warn him a little late, because it's been so long you're caught off guard by how fast and enthusiastically your body reacts.

"You can come," he murmurs, as though giving permission, and by God you do.

You come as though release has been bottled up inside you for years. Which, technically, no. But a bicycle built for two is so much better, even if Riordan watches you arch and pant and spill with a faint, knowledgeable smile.

When he finally lets you lower your arms, your legs are shaking so badly you can barely stand up. He turns you to the bookshelf, and you hang onto it for dear life, eyes locked on the words *Wildfire at Midnight*.

The phrase seems weirdly portentous. You can't seem to get past it as Riordan's fingers slip along your crack, and then pierce you with slow, deliberate intent. You shudder, but it's not rejection. Spent though you are, you don't want the connection to end.

He's got something slick and silky on his fingers. Is that...? Or did he bring something?

Wild...fire...at...mid...night...

Riordan's finger presses in, pulls out, presses in, pushes further. It feels good, that friction. You moan.

"It's been a while," he remarks. He kisses the curve of your shoulder and continues to explore all your little nooks and crannies by press and push and prod. By the time he finishes, you're flushed and breathless with anticipation — and yes, maybe a little anxiety. You don't have to wait long.

Riordan spreads your ass cheeks and pushes in. He gives a little groan.

"Jesus fucking Christ. That's nice." One of his hands is locked on your hip. The other rubs your belly. Does he think you bring good luck to the wearer? It hasn't worked that way so far.

You're not sure you can take him without splitting apart, but since that's not an option, your body — and mind — submit, sphincter muscle spasming around his stiffness as he shoves the rest of the way in.

"Okay?" he asks in that rough, unsteady voice. He gives a little instinctive thrust.

You nod. You give an instinctive push back.

The side door swings open and you both freeze.

No mistake. The side door to the building is open. Someone has picked the lock and slipped into the building. The night scent of the city pours in on a draft of cold air — and with it a hint of something else. Gasoline?

Terrifying. And embarrassing. Mostly terrifying. Although Riordan's reaction seems to be mostly rage. He pulls out of you — ouch — and shoves you down. "Stay here, baby."

He yanks his pants up and he's in pursuit. Granted, a slightly stiff-legged pursuit, but he's moving with speed and purpose through the canyons of bookshelves.

You don't stay put, of course. You get up and move after Riordan, more slowly and more cautiously — and stopping to grab the perfectly real poker from the faux fireplace.

You catch up to Riordan in time to see him tackle a tall masked figure in a raincoat. The figure drops what he's carrying, which turns out to be a gasoline can.

The two men go crashing into one of the bookshelves, which creates a domino effect around the room, shelf after shelf crashing into each other.

The man in the raincoat whips out a gigantic and very sharp-looking knife. Riordan wrests it from him, and then stabs him through the shoulder, pinning the man in the raincoat to the bookshelf.

Not like in the movies, that's for sure.

The man stops fighting and begins screaming. Riordan rips off the scary skeleton mask, and you both gasp.

It's Bruce Green.

The reporter from *Boytimes* is your stalker.

It turns out that Green is more than a stalker. After he's arrested and interrogated, he confesses to murdering Robert. You were next on his list.

Bruce is tried but found not guilty by reason of insanity. He's sent to the loony bin and continues to write you weekly letters, which you save to share at his eventual sanity hearing. Meantime Detective Riordan is forced to resign from the police department which takes a dim view of his having "social relations" with a suspect in a murder case. "Social" may have been a typo.

Anyway, Riordan quits the force and opens an Irish pub not far from Cloak and Dagger books.

You continue to see each other "socially" every chance you get — and you get *a lot* of chances.

The End

After you hang up, another idea occurs to you. You look up the number for *Boytimes* and give them a call, but no one at *Boytimes* has ever heard of Bruce Green.

So that's definitely weird.

Good thing you didn't make the mistake of talking to him.

You get the owners of the Thai restaurant next door to help you lift the bookshelves upright and you spend the rest of the evening putting books away and carrying broken records and smashed glass to the dumpster in the alley.

When you're done, you drag yourself upstairs, take the phone off the hook, and fall into bed.

When you open your eyes your bedroom is full of white mist.

Fire! you think, not unreasonably mistaking all that swirling pale vapor for smoke. You leap out of bed, feeling your way to the door, but after a few steps, the bone-chilling damp of the room stops you in your tracks.

There is no fire.

There is no warmth in the entire building. You might as well be standing outside. In fact...you peer through the shape-shifting fog. You can't see the door at all, and your dresser looks more like...a hedge. With white berries.

Weird and weirder.

You must have left a window open. But when you turn to the window, you can't make it out at all. You walk toward where the window should be, and your feet sink into the soft, spongy ground. Wait. Wait. This is too weird. The floorboards are gone and you're standing in wet grass.

You take another step forward and not only is the window gone, the walls of your room look more like the crumbled walls of an ancient building.

A small, square building.

A tomb.

Okay. You're dreaming, so no need to panic.

You should probably take control by getting back in bed, closing your eyes, and thinking of something pleasant.

But when you turn around there's no sign of your bed. Or your bedroom. Or Cloak and Dagger Books. Or Pasadena.

What the...?

The hedge to your left rustles loudly, and you whirl around in time to see a man and woman in long black capes gliding toward you. There's something vaguely familiar about them — or there would be if they weren't...

No. It has to be the light.

They can't really be...purple. Can they?

You stare more closely. The man is, yes, purple, but aside from that, he's elderly, medium height, spare build.

He has thinning jet-black hair and a pencil-thin mustache. You know you've seen him before. But where?

The woman is, yes, purple, middle-aged, portly, with a mild expression and frizzy dark hair.

Then it clicks. These two were with that bus tour that showed up at your shop this morning. The two you found wandering around your living quarters.

Except they weren't purple this morning. And they didn't have flowing capes. And they weren't gliding eerily through the mists.

You take a couple of steps back as they skate toward you.

"Can I help you?" you ask.

They answer, but it's hard to understand them because they speak in a kind of hiss. Actually, it's hard to understand them because those fangs — like snake fangs — are all you can think about. Those are two sets of scary teeth. It's difficult to concentrate on anything else as they continue toward you, making that clicking, hissing noise.

"Okay. Stop." You hold up your hands, index fingers crossed like in a...cross. Yes, you feel completely silly because this has got to be a dream, right? You've been having some very weird dreams lately. And they're purple, after all. The vampires, not your dreams. Though some of your dreams are admittedly purple.

But getting back to the vampires, with that skin tone they could be related to Count von Count. For all you know they just want to help you with your bookkeeping.

Maybe the crossed fingers work because the vampires pause about arm's length from you.

"Where ith it?" the lady vampire says.

"Where ith what?" You lick your teeth. "Where *is* what?"

"The Croth of Ruin," the older vampire says in an older crotchety vampire voice.

"I truly have no idea what you're talking about."

This is not the answer they want and they bare their fangs and hiss more loudly.

"I don't recognize that title," you protest. "Do you know who wrote it? Who's the publisher? ISBN number? Work with me."

"Ith not a book!" the lady vampire snarls. Well, it's a lisping sort of snarl. She gets the point across. She rakes her claws at you — she's wearing purple nail polish too — but she doesn't touch you. So the crossed fingers must work. Good to know.

"Well, this is a bookstore," you tell her. At least it was when you went to bed. It does appear to be a ruined tomb in the middle of a forest now, but still. "If it's a DVD or a CD, I can direct you to —"

They're practically fizzing with frustration now and they are both making little lunges at you. This time one of the lady vampire's long purple fingernails rakes your wrist.

"Hey!" You stare down at the dots of blood.

"You think to keep it for yourthelf!" snarls the old vampire.

"I don't even know what it ith. *Is*."

"The Croth of Ruin!" They shriek at you in unison.

"I heard you the firth time," you yell back. "I don't know what that is."

For some minutes now you've been aware of a growling sound in the distance. The growl grows louder and louder and you recognize the purr of a powerful engine. About the same time you make the connection, a black-garbed figure roars up on a gleaming motorcycle the size of a small silver buffalo.

A large man leaps from the motorcycle and whips out two gleaming, razor sharp butterfly swords. He briskly spins them over his head and shoulders in a complicated choreographed move and then advances on the two vampires who fall back, cowering behind their raised capes.

"Stand aside, Sir English," the man commands. "I've got this."

You peer at him more closely.

He looks a *lot* like Detective Riordan except he's dressed all in black leather beneath one of those soft, swirly, wool duster coats. His hair is a little longer than Riordan's and he's wearing an eyepatch.

"Who are you supposed to be?" you inquire. Clearly you have got to stop eating cheese before bedtime.

"Professor Janick Von Riesling. Vampire Slayer," he throws over his shoulder.

"Isn't your last name supposed to be Van Helsing?" you ask doubtfully.

"You drink what you like, I'll drink what I like." Von Riesling sets off in pursuit of the vampires who are gliding away at top speed, still sputtering and sizzling their discontent.

This is a very exhausting dream. You sit down on the wall of the tomb and close your eyes. Whatever happened to nice normal nightmares about showing up for finals after missing six weeks of all your college courses? Or giving a speech and realizing you're naked? No, you've got to have these complicated supernatural...

"That's that," Von Riesling says briskly right next to you, and you sit up straight, realizing that you were falling asleep again. Of course you're already asleep so...it's kind of confusing. "Good thing I was in time," Von Riesling adds.

You nod. He really looks a lot like Detective Riordan. Except Detective Riordan doesn't usually gaze at you with that sort of speculative glint in his eyes. Eye.

Or does he?

"Here, let me give you a hand," Von Riesling says gallantly, slipping an arm around you and lifting you to your feet.

"What happened to your other eye?" you ask.

"Nothing. I think it looks more formidable, that's all."

"Oh."

He pushes the eyepatch back. His eyes are green. So green they almost seem to glow as he gazes intently into your eyes, and his mouth is coming ever closer to yours. In fact, his lips are only a kiss away when you start to say, "You know, you look ecthackly like —"

His mouth covers yours in a kiss so deliciously sweet it seems to stop your heart in your chest. You kiss him back, harder. You can't seem to get enough of him.

"Ow!" Von Riesling's hands fasten on your biceps and he pushes you back. "Did you just bite me?"

You blush and lick your lip. You do taste a hint of copper on your tongue. You put a hand to your mouth, and wow your teeth are sharp. You don't remember your incisors ever being quite so pointy.

"Thorry," you murmur.

"No biting," Von Riesling warns you. "No teeth. No scratching either."

You nod. He leans in to kiss you again. Oh, it's even nicer the second time. He tastes lovely and he's *such* a good kisser. This is the nicest dream you've had in ages...

"Oh thit!" Von Riesling says suddenly.

THE END

You grab your keys, wallet, and jacket and head down the stairs. But when you reach the ground floor and try to open the side entrance, it sticks. You wiggle the handle, then tug on it, then brace your feet and haul with all your might, but it won't budge.

You find the WD-40 in the stock room and spray it over the lock and the handle, but it's no use. The door remains as firmly sealed as though someone had bricked over the entrance.

The phone upstairs is ringing again.

You give up and try the front entrance. To your relief, the glass door opens normally. But when you try to slide the security gate aside, it won't move.

You grab the bars and start shaking them like James Cagney in one of those old prison flicks. What the heck is going on?

The phone upstairs continues to ring. Destiny calling.

If you choose to answer the phone,
turn to page 133

If you choose to answer the phone,
turn to page 133

If you choose to answer the phone,
turn to page 133

If you choose to answer the phone,
turn to page 133

ACKNOWLEDGEMENTS

Sincere thanks to K.B. Smith and Keren.

Thank you also to those of you who have written through the years expressing your love for the Adrien books. There is nothing more gratifying for any author than knowing your work has touched the lives of so many. You're very kind.

Not everyone will be delighted with the liberties taken in this book. I will simply remind you that no one has a better sense of humor than Adrien. He would be delighted with this book, although he would object strenuously to the lack of choices in a number of scenarios.

Some of Adrien's dream sequence dead ends are in fact literary mash-ups of the following public domain works:

Slaves of the Dust by Sophie Wenzel Ellis,
Astounding Stories, 1930.

The Sunken Empire by H. Thompson Rich,
Astounding Stories, 1931.

The Gate to Xoran by Hal K. Wells,
Astounding Stories, 1931.

Sign of the Spider by Bertram Mitford, 1896.

Finally, thank you, YOU, for buying this book.

ABOUT THE AUTHOR

A distinct voice in gay fiction, multi-award-winning author JOSH LANYON has been writing gay mystery, adventure and romance for over a decade. In addition to numerous short stories, novellas, and novels, Josh is the author of the critically acclaimed Adrien English series, including *The Hell You Say*, winner of the 2006 USABookNews awards for GLBT Fiction. Josh is an Eppie Award winner and a three-time Lambda Literary Award finalist.

Follow Josh on Twitter, Facebook, and Goodreads.

Find other Josh Lanyon titles at www.joshlanyon.com

Printed in Great Britain
by Amazon.co.uk, Ltd.,
Marston Gate.